Spiritual Entropy

Life-Changing Insights Revealed by a Unique Natural Law

Gilbert L. Wedekind, Ph.D.

xulon
PRESS

Spiritual Entropy
by Gilbert L. Wedekind, Ph.D.

Printed in the United States of America

Library of Congress Control Number: 2003100571
ISBN 1-591605-59-8

Scripture quotations in this publication are taken from the Holy Bible: New International Version® (NIV®), copyright © 1973, 1978, 1984 by International Bible Society, used by permission of Zondervan Publishing House, all rights reserved; *The New English Bible* (NEB), © 1961, 1970, the Delegates of the Oxford University Press and the Syndics of the Cambridge University Press; used by permission, all rights reserved.

Xulon Press
10640 Main Street
Suite 204
Fairfax, VA 22030
(703) 934-4411
XulonPress.com

To order additional copies, call 1-866-909-BOOK (2665).

To June, my wife and best friend;
to René and Ty, our children;
and to all who would join me in the noble search for truth.

Contents

❧··❧

Acknowledgments

⋙•⋘

Most of the ideas contained in this book were developed over the delightful years that I have been privileged to be a teacher. Many different people have encouraged and inspired me through the years. Gordon Van Wylen deserves special thanks for sparking my initial thinking on the subject over thirty-five years ago.

For a number of years now, I have been presenting these developing ideas to groups of people of different ages and backgrounds. I am grateful for their enthusiastic and encouraging response to these presentations. It has been a prime source of motivation for writing the book.

I am also grateful for the valuable feedback and encouragement given to me by all the people who have read the manuscript. Their backgrounds represent a variety of disciplines—the humanities, the arts, the sciences, medicine, engineering, law, and theology. I hesitate to name some for fear of discounting the contributions of others. Nevertheless, I must recognize Bob Davis, and Pat Karbowski, who, because of their level of involvement, have had considerable influence on the developing manuscript.

Very special thanks go to Barb Oakley and Eric Stanford for the unique contributions of their individual editorial insights. In sequence, they patiently and skillfully helped me transform the material into a form that is more reader-friendly.

Finally, I want to thank my wife, June. She has been responsible for most of the word processing. But her contribution goes far beyond that. As my best friend and companion in this great adventure of life, she is an integral part in the many personal stories I tell in the book. Without her patience, love, and encouragement, this work could never have been completed.

Introduction

⋙·⋘

Each of the natural laws of science has something valuable to tell us about the physical universe and our existence within it. Whether we are talking about the laws that govern the formation of crystals, the laws that govern the release of nuclear energy within a star, or the laws that govern the flow of air around an airplane's wing, each natural law adds another brick to the edifice of our knowledge about the way the universe operates. But there is one fundamental natural law that seems to go beyond all the others in its meaning for our lives. Since the discovery of this law in the nineteenth century, scientists and other thinkers have believed they have seen it at work both in individual lives and in human society. This very special law is technically called "the second law of thermodynamics," or more popularly, "the entropy law."

If entropy, as a concept, is new to you, not to worry. The chapters that follow, especially chapters two through five, will explain it at some length, both within the context of thermodynamics (the study of energy) and in terms of everyday life experience. For now, what is important to know is that "the entropy law" describes the observed natural tendency of all things to go from a state of greater order to a state of lesser order—the word "entropy" being a measure of the disorder.[1] Why does a room tend to get messy instead of spontaneously clean itself up? Why do cars periodically need repair rather than always working perfectly? Why do batteries run down instead of charging themselves up? We might never stop to ask ourselves such questions; it just seems natural to us for houses to become messy, cars to break down, and battery power to drop. But that's the point: there is a fundamental natural law operating here, and it is the second law of thermodynamics. Entropy may not be something you know much about from a scientific standpoint, but you do know about it on all kinds of personal levels.

Our personal, everyday experience of the second law of thermodynamics in the physical world is remarkable enough. What is even more remarkable is that this law, or its analogy, appears to hold true in realms that are not normally covered by the laws of physics at all. Why does a message tend to get garbled as it is passed along? Entropy seems to operate in the realm of information transfer. Why does a couple's relationship tend to become strained if they don't keep working at their marriage? Entropy appears to operate in social situations. Why do we get stressed out when we are overworked? Entropy appears to work in the psychological domain. This book will touch on the operation of entropy in these kinds of human experiences. But that is not the central contribution of this book; other writers have talked about some of those kinds of entropy. This book has an agenda that is more profound, going after answers to some of the ultimate questions of our existence. It explores what entropy may be able to reveal to us about the moral, the spiritual, and the sacred. It dares to ask, what can entropy tell us about God?

Here are a few of the intriguing questions this book will

explore in its later chapters, after laying a foundation for understanding entropy:

- What does entropy have to contribute to the controversial debate about origins and "intelligent design"?
- What, if anything, does entropy have to do with the disturbing truth that people often treat each other badly?
- How can an individual overcome "ethical entropy" in his or her own life?
- How does entropy correspond with the teachings of the world's religious scriptures, particularly the Bible?
- What hope do we have that one day we may be able to live free from the detrimental effects of entropy?

These are tremendously significant questions—and ones we can reasonably hope to find answers to. The unique law of entropy is even capable of giving us unique insights into our spiritual condition.

But perhaps you are already balking. *When it comes to exploring God and spirituality, aren't we asking entropy to do too much?* you may be wondering. That's a question you will have to answer for yourself. But I would ask you to open your mind to the possibilities. I would ask you to come along with me on a voyage of discovery and see if perhaps entropy can change the paradigms by which you see life.[2]

The Invisible Framework

Paradigm is a buzzword heard often these days. Businesspeople speak of marketing paradigms; corporate executives have their management paradigms; and engineers use design paradigms. The word is derived from the Greek word *paradeigma,* meaning "model." Of course, we all know what a model is. It can be a small-scale replica, such as a model car, boat, or airplane. Or it can be an example, such as a model house, a fashion model, or even a role model. It can also be a description or explanation, such as a weather forecasting model, an economic model, or a scientific or engineering model. Our paradigms, then, serve us as useful approximations to reality.

It is hard to overestimate the value of paradigms. They represent examples, patterns, and rules. They provide insight and understanding. They have predictive capability. Without paradigms, we would be unable to reason, entertain rational thoughts, or make what we like to think are intelligent decisions. Paradigms are not only important—they are essential to life as we know it.

Yet in spite of their great value, paradigms have a downside. This downside is related to the fact that multiple and even conflicting paradigms can be associated with the same subject. And such subjects can be important ones, running the gamut of human activities and concerns—work, family, money, friendship, sex, ethics, death, sin, origins, religion, and God. We all have some sort of paradigm for these subjects. But as I have said, our paradigms are only models—*approximations* to reality. We put ourselves at risk when we think our paradigm on a particular subject is both complete and correct, when in fact it may be neither.

So a question arises. My paradigms represent my current understanding of important and diverse subjects. I use these paradigms every day to generate my rational thought and make life-influencing decisions. How, then, do I know whether my personal paradigms on these subjects are valid approximations of reality?

There is no easy way to answer this crucial question. A piece of the answer, however, lies in the integrity of the source of our paradigms. Where did we get them? Television? The Internet? Movies? Books? Newspapers? Friends? Teachers? Parents? Examined evidence? Hearsay? A self-appointed spiritual leader? Another piece of the answer lies in what kind of effort we have invested in evaluating whether our paradigm on a particular subject is simply someone else's opinion or instead is based upon reasoned evidence.

In science and engineering, the validity of a model or paradigm can be judged by how well it agrees with experimental data. It is not so easy to judge nonscientific paradigms. But life itself, through the crucible of family, friendships, and even adverse situations, can serve as a sort of testing process. We can also learn from the experiences of others. In fact, the quality of others' lives can serve as a trustworthy indication of the value of certain paradigms, against which we can evaluate our own paradigms. The best situation, if such were to exist, would be to have a trustworthy source for at least some of the more important paradigms, which we could then use as standards against which we could calibrate all our own paradigms.

But in all this, the point to remember is that paradigms act as information filters. As one commentator says, "What we actually perceive is determined by our paradigms. What may be perfectly visible, perfectly obvious, to persons with one paradigm, may be quite literally invisible to persons with a different paradigm."[3] A classic example of the filtering role of paradigms took place within the world of Swiss watch making.

In 1970, the Swiss dominated the worldwide watchmaking industry with over 60 percent of the market. By the early 1980s, their share of the market had dropped to 10 percent. Why? The quartz electronic watch.

Who invented the quartz watch? The Indonesians? The Germans? The Japanese? No. Actually, the quartz watch was conceived by the Swiss themselves. It was invented in 1967 at the Swiss Watch Federation Research Center in Neufchatel, Switzerland. The inventors presented it to Swiss manufacturers, who rejected it. Not having any details of the discussion, we can only guess at their comments. Perhaps they said: "It doesn't tick. It has no gears or jeweled bearings. How could it even be considered a watch?" Their paradigm—the traditional watch—blinded them to the truth, and the rest is history.[4]

You can see how effectively our paradigms can trap us into seeing the world in only one way, and how wrong even the experts can be because of that entrapment.

Because we have freedom of choice, many of the paradigms that make up our view of the world are those paradigms that we, for whatever reason, have decided are important. The big question is, of course, how closely do our paradigms relate to the *truth* about life? I don't know about you, but the thought that I might be blind to the truth about some subject because of preconceived ideas, or erroneous paradigms, is a bit scary to me. This fear is probably a good thing, however, because it gives me good reason to all the more carefully examine the paradigms that filter my view of the world and influence the important decisions I make.

Some of the ideas and concepts in the upcoming chapters will be familiar to you, but I am sure that many others will be new to you. One thing, however, is certain. As you encounter them, you will filter those ideas and thoughts through your existing paradigms. Hopefully, in many cases, the ideas will find a logical place within some of your existing fundamental paradigm structures. However, on some occasions, you may find that your existing paradigms are in conflict with an idea or concept you encounter within these pages. If this happens, I urge you not to impulsively reject the idea, without giving both the idea and the validity of your own conflicting paradigms reasoned thought.

One valuable byproduct of your reading this book can be that you will become more aware of your paradigms and begin making adjustments to conform them more closely to the truth as you discover it. The subject of entropy, perhaps surprisingly to many, can be a most useful catalyst in this all-important process.

Why Investigate Spiritual Entropy?

If I appear to belabor the importance of being open to adjusting one's paradigms, it is not only because the spiritual implications I will later on draw from the natural law of entropy are so *astounding* to so *many;* it is also because those implications are so *important* to one person—*you.* The conclusions that I will present for your consideration, if correct, have the potential to change your view of God, the way you live your life, and even the condition of your soul. In short, there is personal meaning to all this; our journey of discovery, though it may begin in our heads, should not end there. I can assure you, from personal experience, that this is true.

Throughout my professional career in science, I have wrestled with understanding entropy. Sometimes I might have liked to restrict my focus to the scientific meaning of this law, yet its more far-reaching implications would inevitably intrude on my thinking. So at an early point I made what I hoped then and still believe was a courageous decision: I chose to pursue the truth of entropy wherever it led me. (It has led me to discoveries both remarkable and profound.) And thus, the theme of entropy has been interwoven in the fabric of my life since my student days, as you will very shortly learn in chapter one, and it has changed my life. That is why I have confidence that you, too, if you will hold your paradigms open to revision, may find this book not merely interesting but life changing.

I'll say it again: come along with me as we explore together the meaning for our lives of *spiritual entropy.*

1

Mind Flood:
A Scientist's Encounter with Supernatural Inspiration

Eureka! I have found it!
—*Archimedes (287–212 b.c.)*

Although I had heard about this kind of thing, I had never before personally experienced anything like it. It went on, as well as I can recall, for about fifteen minutes. Then, as suddenly as it had begun, it stopped. When I glanced down at my watch, I found it was shortly after midnight.

That quarter-hour experience, occurring more than thirty-five years ago, has had a profound influence on my life. It has shaped my professional career, my academic focus, and in many ways my perception of life itself. But already I am ahead of myself. Let me take you back in time with me to set the scene.

Hitting the Wall

It was early April 1965. In Urbana, Illinois, where I lived, the nights were still cool, but the days were beginning to warm under the influence of a determined Midwestern sun. My wife, June, and I occupied a small home on the southeastern edge of the community with cornfields on two sides of us. Those fields had just been plowed in readiness for spring planting, and the sweet aroma of the rich, black soil wafted into our windows each evening as we tucked ourselves into bed.

As a doctoral candidate at the University of Illinois School of Engineering, I was at that time totally immersed in my research. This research was in an area known by the heavy-handed name of "two-phase evaporating flow phenomena." More specifically, my research was centered on something called the "liquid-dry-out point." I won't bore you with the details, but an understanding of liquid dry-out is important to the design and safety of conventional and nuclear power plants.

I had spent over a year developing an experimental test facility, winding electrical heating tape on glass tubes, sweat-soldering copper fittings, installing pumps, hooking up heat exchangers, and fiddling with flowmeters and pressure sensors. A high-speed movie camera was used to record the behavior of the liquid-dry-out point (technically, the "transient behavior"). When I had finished building and checking out the experimental apparatus, I had gone on to spend another five months running many different experiments to study the dry-out point's behavior over a wide range of operating conditions. The experiments were repeatable, and I was convinced the measurements were accurate, but the ultimate goal of my research was to use the experimental observations as insight for developing a theoretical model—a model that, with equations, would draw a picture of the behavior of the liquid-dry-out point similar to what I was capturing with my movie camera.

That's where I hit the wall—a high, formidable wall with no apparent openings.

A Picture in My Mind

To understand what I mean about hitting the wall, you first have to understand how doctoral programs work.

Doctoral students generally have committees made up of four or five professors, one of whom is the chairperson. Usually the chairperson is the principal adviser for your research. My doctoral committee was made up of five professors—three from mechanical engineering, one from math, and one from theoretical and applied mechanics. The doctoral committee has the power of life and death over your thesis.

Among your many tasks as a doctoral student, it is your responsibility to convince the committee that the research you are proposing to do has never been done before and has long-term value. But that's only the beginning. Then you actually have to make it happen. The end product has to be a "significant piece of research." Significant, at least, to the doctoral committee. At the University of Illinois, Champaign-Urbana, doctoral committees had a high estimation of what the word *significant* meant.

The wall I hit was my inability to come up with a mathematically solvable theoretical model, and the reason for this failure was the complexity of the interactions of the many physical processes involved.

I had a real problem. If I could not come up with a model that successfully described what I was observing experimentally, I would have to abandon this particular research project and start all over again on a new one. After having spent more than a year and a half of my life on this research, the thought of abandoning it and starting all over was not pleasant. In fact, I was becoming desperate. Sometimes my wife and I would talk about the situation into the early hours of the morning.

A month went by. What I really needed was some new insight. A new way of looking at what was going on physically. In essence, a better picture of the most important physical processes controlling what I was seeing. I worked and worked at it, but with no success.

Another month went by. Still no new insight. No new picture.

Then late one evening I was sitting in my office at the

university. In what could only be described as a discouraged state of mind, I was staring at the pages of my existing model (my paradigm), trying to find some form of error—conceptual, logical, or mathematical. My office mate, a tireless, late-night individual, had left an hour or so earlier. The building was as quiet as a museum after hours. Perhaps I was its only occupant. I don't even recall hearing any crickets outside the office window.

Then it happened. All of a sudden, a brand-new idea invaded my mind. It began with a simple picture: a line drawing. I knew it was not something I had ever thought about before. Then, in the wake of the picture, a sequence of thoughts began flooding through my mind. I began writing them down on a tablet of lined yellow paper. The thoughts were coming so fast that my cramping fingers could hardly keep up. I remember wishing that the train of thoughts streaming into my mind would slow down so that I would not miss anything.

The experience went on for nearly a quarter-hour, as well as I can recall. Then, as suddenly as it had begun, it stopped. When I went back over what I had written down, I recognized that I had been given an idea for a very different approach to solving my problem.

Before leaving that night, I was able, using this different approach, to put together a mathematical model, albeit somewhat crude, for predicting the transient behavior of the liquid-dry-out point. I plugged numbers into the model and found that it predicted my experimental observations with substantial accuracy. That is, the picture it drew of the liquid-dry-out point behavior was nearly identical to what I had photographed. I was ecstatic. I could hardly wait to get home and share with my wife the excitement of what I had experienced.

Over a period of several weeks, I reformulated the new theoretical model into a more acceptable form. With it, I found I could successfully predict all of the experimental data I had collected over the previous six months. Although the data involved a great variety of experiments, with widely varying physical parameters and operating conditions, in virtually every case the theoretical predictions were in good agreement with my real-life observations. The conceptual ideas in the successful model were considerably different from those in the earlier model—a significant paradigm adjustment.

During the following years, I have applied that same theoretical model to a wide variety of related problems with equally successful results. In fact, in the technical literature the model has become known as the "System Mean Void Fraction Model." Over that same time period, I have received a number of scientific research grants from the National Science Foundation and have written over two dozen technical papers on the subject—papers that have been published in national and international journals. I have also been invited to a number of technical conferences to present my research findings. All of this research has utilized the System Mean Void Fraction Model—the model given to me that night so many years ago as I sat in my office at the University of Illinois. Even now, over three decades later, this gift continues to impact my life.[1]

The Other Paradigm Shift

That short but dramatic experience has had a profound effect on my life, not just professionally, but in every other respect. I have had many years to think about what happened that night. I have also had other experiences in which something happened to me that I cannot account for in strictly naturalistic terms (you will hear about some of them later on in this book). As a result of these experiences, as well as years of reflection and thought, I have arrived at what I believe are a number of valuable insights into what was happening late that April evening so many years ago.

It seems to me that the gift of insight I received could only have come from above. My own thinking up to that point did not lead to this radically different analytical approach. No one else told me about it. So where else could it have come from but a supernatural source? It's hard for me to convey this to you, but the sense I had that God was involved was undeniable. I did not doubt it then; I do not doubt it now.

I had before this time been willing to believe in the existence of God. But I thought of him as being an impersonal force. He did not really figure much in my scientific thinking or research. I recognize now that the most important paradigm shift that took place that night was not my new insight into the liquid-dry-out point but the change that began in my thinking about God. It has led to a spiritual adventure that I would not trade for anything.

And this brings us to entropy. Entropy (a physical effect that will be explored in more detail in the next chapter) was a factor I had to take into account in my research into two-phase evaporating flow phenomena. In fact, the entropy law was the basis for one of the key elements in my System Mean Void Fraction Model. And shortly after the mind flood I have described, I remembered having read something in a textbook about the second law of thermodynamics. That textbook happened to mention in passing that entropy has philosophical implications that reach far beyond science. Undoubtedly because I had become much more spiritually attuned as a result of my experience that one late night, this comment now lodged deeply in my mind. I determined that, as my career in engineering unfolded, I would do my best to tease out those other implications.

This book is the fruit of that career-long search. I have come to believe that there *is* such a thing as spiritual

24

entropy, and it has everything to do with a God who cares about normal human beings like me—and like you.

2

Why Ice Cream Melts:
An Introduction to Thermodynamics, the Science of Energy

Gather ye rosebuds while ye may,
Old Time is still aflying,
And this same flower that smiles today,
Tomorrow will be dying.
—Robert Herrick (1591–1674)

"It's water over the dam."
"My 'get up and go' got up and went."
"Time waits for no man."

I'm sure you are familiar with each of these adages and many more like them. But have you ever considered what they have in common? They all imply that time, with its flow of events, moves irreversibly in a single direction. This directionality is described in science by a fundamental natural law known as *the second law of thermodynamics.*

Now, don't get worried. This is not a textbook on science, and it won't be giving a detailed study of thermodynamics. Instead, it will focus on insights about life that we can glean from this "second law"—the law of entropy.

The special contribution of this book is in the *spiritual* implications of the entropy law. But before we get to spiritual entropy, we first must understand physical entropy. And perhaps the easiest way to begin that task is with the help of before-and-after contrasts. A series of such contrasts is listed below. As you read and visualize them, pay particular attention to the natural direction of the physical processes that take place.

- A dining room just before guests arrive for a dinner party; the same room just after the last guest leaves
- A brand-new car driven off the showroom floor; the same car ten years later
- A rock overhanging the side of a mountain just before it breaks off; the same rock several minutes later
- A dry pine forest just prior to a lightning strike; the same forest the next morning
- A bowl of soup too hot to eat; the same soup five minutes later (three if you blow on it)
- The skin on the face of newborn child; the same face seventy years later
- An ice cream cone just after it was served to you on a warm summer evening; the same cone five minutes later if you have not licked it

In what direction did the physical conditions in these examples naturally go? What *is* the cause of ice cream melting? The second law of thermodynamics provides answers to questions like these. And to understand that law, we must consider it within the overarching discipline of science called thermodynamics.

The Conservation of Energy Principle

Thermodynamics is the study of energy in all its many forms. A simple definition for energy is that it is "the capacity to produce change."

Consider the capacity to produce change in *chemical* energy—for example, the change that can be produced by gunpowder, gasoline, or dynamite. Or consider the change that can be produced by the *thermal* energy found in boiling water, molten lava, or a campfire. Or consider the changes wrought by the *nuclear* energy in a nuclear reactor or a nuclear bomb. Remember the overhanging rock on the side of a mountain, about to break off? That's *gravitational* energy. A speeding automobile out of control is filled with *kinetic* energy. The nearest electrical outlet in your house waits for you to plug in some appliance, which needs *electrical* energy. Each of these different forms of energy represents the capacity to produce change.

Thermodynamics is also the study of the effects that energy transfers and transformations have on substances, processes, devices, and systems. The foundation of any such study is represented by two fundamental principles, known as the first and second laws of thermodynamics. The first law (also called the "conservation of energy principle") states that energy cannot be created or destroyed. It can be *transferred* from one place to another place (such as the transfer of thermal energy from the hot flame on a stove to water in a pan) or it can be *transformed* from one form to another form (such as the burning of gasoline, which is a transformation from chemical energy to thermal energy). The conservation of energy principle, however, states that after an energy transfer or transformation has occurred, the total amount of energy remaining in the universe, regardless of its form or where it is located, is the same as it was to begin with.

Here is an analogy that may be helpful: Consider all of the earth's gold. Some of it—perhaps most of it—is still buried beneath of the earth's surface in the form of gold ore. It also exists in the form of gold bars (in this country, they are stored in vaults at Fort Knox, Kentucky). Gold is also present in the form of coins and jewelry. If gold cannot be created or destroyed, then—although gold bars or coins can be transferred to another geographical location or melted down and transformed into jewelry—the total amount of gold on the earth remains the same.

This holds true for energy as well; that's what we learn from the first law of thermodynamics.

Yet as significant as the first law of thermodynamics is,

it is important for us to note that it has some limitations in its ability to provide insights about energy. For example, the first law does not give us any information about the degree of completeness, or the efficiency, that might be possible for any energy transformation process (such as the efficiency of the engine in your car, which is related to the distance you can travel on a known quantity of gasoline). Nor does the first law give us any clue as to whether a particular process is physically possible or not. For example, our before-and-after situations represent naturally occurring processes that go in only one direction—hanging rocks fall and hot soup cools, ice cream melts and human skin ages. The reverse can never occur naturally. But the first law tells us nothing about this.

It is the second law of thermodynamics that provides insight into what energy transformation efficiencies are possible and also what natural processes may occur.

The Entropy Principle

Each before-and-after situation that was described earlier (the melting ice cream cone and so on) involved a process of deterioration in physical order. The direction was always the same—a natural tendency to go from order toward disorder. These before-and-after situations are specific, observable examples of the second law's influence.

A subtler characteristic that the before-and-after situations have in common is the transfer or transformation of energy. For example, the cooling of the hot soup and the melting of the ice cream both involve a heat transfer. Thermal energy always flows from a higher-temperature object to a lower-temperature object. So we see that in our examples the hot soup gave up energy to the cooler air and the cold ice cream received energy from the warmer air. The burning of the forest and the oxidation of the paint and metals in a car involved a transformation of energy from one form to another at the molecular level. These naturally occurring energy transfers and transformations consistently resulted in an overall deterioration in the value, or usefulness, of the energy being transferred or transformed. Furthermore, when an energy transfer or transformation took place, some percentage of that energy became unavailable for use in the way it could be used before the energy transfer or transformation. The energy was not destroyed, but its usefulness was diminished.

Stay with me while we consider another example: heating a house with natural gas during the winter. The burning of the natural gas results in the transformation of chemical energy into thermal energy in the furnace. This energy in turn is transferred to the air inside the house. Because the air temperature inside the house is warmer than the outside air temperature, thermal energy is transferred from inside the house to the outside air. Although insulation slows the thermal energy transfer, it cannot completely stop it.

At the end of the winter heating season, this is what we would observe: First, we would see that the amount of energy in the universe has not changed (first law). The energy that previously existed in the form of chemical energy in the natural gas still exists, but it would now be in the form of low-temperature thermal energy, either within the earth (or its atmosphere) or in outer space. Although it would still exist as thermal energy, none of the energy that was initially used to heat the house would be available for further use (all consequences of the second law). Therefore, the energy that was initially in the natural gas would have deteriorated in its value to us.

Whether it is obvious or subtle, what is common to all of the before-and-after situations is the concept of deterioration. This naturally occurring deterioration is a direct manifestation of the second law of thermodynamics.

Recognizing that a special word was needed to describe

a measure of this disorder and deterioration of energy, the German physicist, Rudolf Clausius, coined the word *entropy* back in 1865.[1] Entropy, like energy, is a conceptual quantity. Also like energy, entropy can be considered a property of a substance or of a system made up of several substances. Again like energy, the entropy (disorder) of a system is the sum of the entropies (disorders) of all its parts. Clausius defined *entropy* in a manner such that the entropy of an isolated system can never decrease without violating the second law. (An isolated system is totally isolated from its surroundings, meaning that no mass or energy can be added to, or removed from, the system.)

In terms of entropy, therefore, the second law of thermodynamics might be stated as "all naturally occurring processes take place in a direction such that the entropy of the universe increases."[2] For this reason, the second law is sometimes referred to as the "entropy law."

Clausius summarized the first and second laws of thermodynamics with the following two statements: "The energy of the universe is constant. The entropy of the universe tends to a maximum."[3]

Local Order, Universal Chaos

The second law of thermodynamics tells us something important about the energy in the universe: its usefulness is running steadily and irreversibly downhill. Yet we need to recognize that it *is* possible, without violating the second law, to decrease the entropy of a localized system by the intelligent use of energy. For example, it is possible to clean up and reorganize the dining room after a dinner party (that is, decrease its entropy), though not without the use of energy and the intellect necessary to distinguish order from disorder. However, after the room has been cleaned, its surroundings will have experienced an *increase* in entropy. Further, the increase in entropy in the surroundings is greater in magnitude than the decrease in entropy in the now-cleaned room.[4] The reason for this is that in addition to the use of human energy, cleaning up the room would most likely have required energy to run the vacuum cleaner, the dishwasher, and the hot water heater—all of which would contribute to an increase in the entropy of the surroundings. These effects, which are consistent with the second law, can be stated more generally like this: "Each localized, man-made or machine-made, entropy decrease is accompanied by a greater increase in entropy of the surroundings, thereby maintaining the required increase in total entropy."[5]

A more natural example in which the entropy of a system can be decreased is found in crystallization. The solidification (changing from a liquid to a solid) of many substances results in the formation of an ordered array of molecules called crystals. Crystals normally have some form of symmetry and are quite beautiful. Water, for instance, begins to crystallize at 32^0 Fahrenheit (0^0 Celsius). Crystallization, including the formation of snowflakes, clearly represents an increase in order. In crystallization, matter is arranging itself into a lower, more stable energy state. Therefore, for crystallization to happen, thermal energy must be removed from the substance. The second law says that whenever thermal energy is transferred out of a substance, the entropy of the substance decreases. So we see that the increase in order represented by crystallization is right in line with what the second law predicts.

One needs, however, to keep in mind the bigger picture. That is, the thermal energy that was transferred out of the substance undergoing crystallization would have to flow into its surroundings, which were at a lower temperature. In its doing so, the second law dictates that the substance's surroundings would experience an increase in entropy that was greater than the decrease in entropy experienced by the substance that was crystallized. Therefore, crystallization results in a net increase in the entropy of the universe.

The second law puts a limit on the efficiency of any energy transformation process and determines whether a particular physical process is possible. But there is more. The faster the process takes place, the lower the efficiency and the greater the amount of entropy produced.

Thus, the second law provides useful insights into the way energy operates. Order can be created within a certain domain, but *always* at the cost of greater disorder in the universe as a whole.

Entropy's Importance

The laws of thermodynamics, as I have described them, are not merely arcane knowledge for a small group of specialists. Rather, they are fundamental laws. Their effects are pervasive in the physical world and thus are important to all scientists.

Albert Einstein once mused over which of the many laws of science deserved to be ranked as the most important law. He is quoted as saying:

> A theory is more impressive with the greater the simplicity of its premises, the more different kinds of things it relates and the more extended its range of applicability. Therefore, the deep impression which classical thermodynamics made on me. It is the only physical theory of universal content which I am convinced, that within the framework of applicability of its basic concepts will never be overthrown.[6]

Einstein's unwavering endorsement of the first and second laws of thermodynamics is all the more significant when we remember that he is most famous for his ability to see beyond the paradigms of the scientific community of his day. His then-controversial theory of relativity significantly altered the existing paradigms regarding the range of applicability of Newtonian mechanics.

The controversial writer Jeremy Rifkin, in a book entitled *Entropy,* agrees with Einstein's assessment of the universal significance of these fundamental laws of thermodynamics.[7] Rifkin calls the second law the supreme law of nature, because of the magnitude of its influence on life and the world around us:

> Once in a great while an idea changes the course of history. The Entropy Law—or the second law of thermodynamics—is such an idea. It states that all energy flows inexorably from the orderly to the disorderly and from the usable to the unusable. According to the Entropy Law, whenever a semblance of order is created anywhere on earth or in the universe, it is done at the expense of causing greater disorder in the surrounding environment. This law was first propounded in the 19th century, but its full implications are only now being felt and explored. Entropy tells us that the world is winding down, and is to the future what the theories of Copernicus and Newton were to the 16th and 17th centuries— a concept both simple and earth-shattering. It is an idea that is already changing the values and goals of philosophers, politicians, scientists, businessmen, and economists. The Entropy Law is about to become an integral part of our world view.[8]

If Rifkin is right on this point, and I believe he is,

entropy is important not only to scientists but to all of us. In fact, entropy is something we all experience and take into account in many ways, whether or not we consciously recognize it for what it is. You might say entropy is like our shadow—it is a dark part of our lives and follows us wherever we go.

3

Our Dark Shadow: The Pervasive Influence of Entropy in Our Lives

> Materialists mistake that which limits life,
> for life itself.
> —*Leo Tolstoy (1828–1910)*

The address was 12 Equestrian Lane. The residence that belonged to that address was the most beautiful house I had ever seen. It could have easily been featured in an issue of *Better Homes & Gardens.*

The time was the early 1950s, and my friend Ernie and I were working for a heating and air conditioning company. We had been sent by our boss to upgrade the air-distribution system servicing the formal living room of 12 Equestrian Lane.

The lady of the house, Mrs. Eleanor Blackstone, met us at the front door. After introducing herself, she asked us to follow her to the living room—and what a living room it was! It was large and bright, with off-white walls and a white shag carpet. In front of the enormous white sectional sofa was a long, highly polished mahogany coffee table, clearly the focal point of the room.

The air-distribution system was in the attic, and the upgrade would require the installation of additional air ducts. When we climbed into the attic, it was obvious that this house was well insulated—at least twelve inches' worth. The insulating material was comprised of expanded mica granules resembling puffed rice cereal. Since the ceiling joists were only eight inches high, there were about four inches of insulation hiding the joists from view, making any movement above the ceiling highly precarious. With a word of caution to Ernie, I went down to the truck to get some tools.

As I walked back into the house, I heard the sound of splintering wood and falling plaster. Hurrying toward the living room, I saw a scene of developing devastation within that once-elegant room. Protruding through the ceiling directly above the coffee table was Ernie's work boot attached to his jeans-clad leg. Flowing around that leg, like a cascading waterfall, was a stream of insulation pellets creating a cone-shaped mountain on top of that beautiful coffee table. The mountain was shrouded in a thick cloud of dust that was rapidly filling the room.

Even while checking to see if Ernie was okay, I was filled with terror at the prospect of explaining all this to Mrs. Blackstone and eventually my boss.

One misstep had transformed this room from a meticulously ordered, low-entropy living room into a chaotic scene of high-entropy devastation. There was also the attendant emotional entropy generated within Ernie, myself, Mrs. Blackstone, and—I can assure you—my boss.[1]

Perhaps there is a general principle here: You can generate a lot of entropy if you are not careful with your next step.

To better understand how intricately and pervasively entropy, the second law of thermodynamics, is involved with our lives, we need to have a broader understanding of its influence.[2] To do this, let's look at its influence in five distinct categories of our physical world: energy resources, time, material objects, environmental pollution, and living things. Along the way, we may learn a few lessons for the wiser living of life.

Entropy at the Flip of a Switch

Political headlines change from day to day, but one subject that has come to public attention in recent decades and shows no sign of going away is energy use. Potential resolutions to any instability in the Middle East are inevitably shaded by what they might do to the flow of oil. People like the lower cost of energy that nuclear power can provide, but they worry about the safety of nuclear power plants. Debates rage over whether we should be drilling for fossil fuels in ecologically sensitive areas or focusing on solutions like increasing conservation and researching alternative fuel sources. These issues really matter because our society is dependent on energy—lots of it and all the time.

This dependency makes us an energy-conscious society. We are interested in news about energy-efficient homes, cars, and appliances. We remind each other to conserve. We even talk about "working smart" rather than just working hard. Perhaps you have heard the story of the recent college graduate who, while interviewing with a potential employer, proudly stated that he would "go through walls" for the company. His words triggered this response from the employer: "No doubt, but would you first think to look for a door?"

Our energy consciousness is a reflection of the second law of thermodynamics. The second law implies that when energy is transferred from one place to another place, or transformed from one form to another form, there is a corresponding deterioration in its quality. The upshot of all this is that high-quality, high-value, usable energy (such as that contained in oil, coal, natural gas, and uranium) is being used up and converted into low-quality, low-value, unusable energy (such as thermal waste, hydrocarbon pollution, and nuclear waste). When we speak of an energy shortage, therefore, the shortage is not in total energy but in high-quality, usable energy.

So while energy use, like Social Security reform, may be one of those perennial issues that raises a yawn when it appears in the back half of a news broadcast, don't expect it to go away. If anything, entropy is slowly pushing it to the forefront of our concerns.

Arrow in Flight

How often, in the midst of your busy schedule, have you said, "Where has all the time gone?" Who has not noticed how time seems to move faster as we grow older? What is it that triggers the sudden awareness of how fast time "flies"? It could have been something as simple as glancing at a clock, a calendar, or a photograph. But in reality, we do not need clocks or calendars to tell us that time has passed—the second law leaves a visible trail as evidence of its passing.

Antique collectors are well aware of this fact and use it as a means of authenticating the age of everything from furniture to letters from Napoleon. Some time ago, I visited a college friend whom I had not seen in many years. He had gone into the business of buying and selling antiques. While showing me his wares, he pointed out a recently acquired piece of furniture. It was handcrafted from beautiful rosewood. The finish, however, was marked with age. Not understanding the world of antique furniture, all I saw were the impressive craftsmanship and gorgeous rosewood. So I commented on how much more beautiful the piece would look if it were refinished. His reply set me straight: "If I refinished it, it would only be worth about a quarter of its present value."

No doubt my friend was correct. Sometimes entropy *can* add value to an item. But only temporarily. It is a certainty that time will eventually destroy my friend's antique, eliminating all its remaining value. That's what happens when entropy is in play.

The familiar adage "Time marches on" conveys the idea

that time goes in the forward direction only. That forward direction is determined by the increase in entropy, which in turn is governed by the second law. For example, if we were watching a video and saw water flowing up a waterfall, or if we saw a rusty iron surface gradually deoxidizing and becoming shiny, we could reasonably conclude that the video was running backward. In the words of Sir Arthur Eddington, "Entropy is time's arrow."[3]

Despite this truth, or perhaps because of it, our so-called "instant society" is caught up with the idea that faster is better, whether we are talking about computers, cars, or appliances. Yet are we doing ourselves a favor by moving faster and faster? The second law clearly indicates that more entropy is generated during fast energy transfers or transformations than when the transfers or transformations are completed more slowly. Therefore, faster is *not* necessarily better, at least as faster relates to the second law, because it results in a greater increase in entropy.

Examples of this truth abound. At the personal level, we could experience this as the difference between the sense of exhaustion we would feel after having run a fast half mile as opposed to having walked a half mile at a leisurely pace. At a national level, we recall how, during the energy crisis of the 1970s, a law was passed reducing the speed limit on interstate highways from seventy to fifty-five miles per hour in order to reduce the amount of fuel (energy) consumption required for a given trip distance.

In fact, this idea that faster is not necessarily better, at least as it relates to the second law, may be applied to any process, device, or system that uses energy in order to function. This is true whether it be an automobile, an appliance, a computer, or a human being. When that same device or system is operated more quickly, the second law sees to it that a greater amount of entropy is generated in completing the task.

Does this have implications for us as individuals and as a society? Think about the "psychological entropy levels" of those of us who continually live on a fast track, with twelve-hour days and seven-day, stress-packed workweeks. There must be some correlation between one's psychological entropy level and one's general health.[4]

Meanwhile, the one commodity that every human being has exactly the same amount of to spend each day is time. This makes time extremely valuable. Most of us use any time-saving devices available to us, with little regard for entropy. We love our microwave ovens, our cell phones, and our PDAs. But we should keep in mind that any savings in time is always counterbalanced by a cost in entropy. And nothing we can do will reverse the direction of time or stop the buildup of entropy.

Toys in the Landfill

Have you ever seen the bumper sticker that declares, "He who has the most toys wins"? Those who choose to decorate their bumpers with the saying may mean it at least partly tongue-in-cheek. Yet it is undeniable that we take pride in our cities, buildings, and houses; our cars, highways, and streets; our appliances, personal computers, and toys of every shape, size, and purpose.

The impact of the second law on material things is significant, as our personal observations and experiences confirm. Cities, buildings, and houses deteriorate; cars rust and wear out, while highways and streets develop chuck holes; appliances malfunction, computers become obsolete, and most, if not all, our toys eventually find their way to some landfill.

For sure, we need some material objects to survive. Others, while not necessary to life, give us genuine pleasure. But those who seek to accumulate more and more "toys" do so only at the expense of much energy and increased entropy. Perhaps in this effect, though, entropy performs a salutary purpose as it causes us to consider the real significance, in the greater scheme of things, of objects we had considered important.

Dirty Foot Tracks

Any homeowner concerned with keeping the house clean knows what a hopeless exercise it is to try to keep dirt from being tracked in (especially if there are kids in the house). It is the same for the human race's "home": planet Earth. We can—and should—do our best to reduce the rate of environmental pollution, just as Mom and Dad can remind the kids to wipe their feet before coming in, but pollution is as inevitable as dirty foot tracks. In fact, the total amount of pollution on our planet's surface and in its atmosphere is destined to increase no matter what we do. The second law says so.

The forms of such environmental pollution are many and common. Neighbors get angry with one another over noise pollution. No city wants nuclear or chemical waste "in their backyard." Beaches are closed when medical waste washes up on shore. Meanwhile, all of us are familiar with the everyday realities of junkyards, "trash mountains," and waste treatment plants.

We live amid our own waste, the pollution produced as a byproduct of human living. And we should not expect this to change. The question can never be whether there will be *any* pollution but rather *how much* pollution. Unless the second law is somehow repealed, there will be pollution as long as there is life or any form of energy transfer or energy transformation.

Life: A Counter-Entropic Force

Like inanimate objects, living things are subject to the influence of the second law. This is true for simple organisms, such as amoebas, as well as for complex organisms, such as flowers, trees, birds, animals, and humans. The natural deterioration of strength, agility, hearing, vision, and general health, leading ultimately to death, is a glaring manifestation of this fact.

Living things do, however, have one advantage over inanimate substances: the life processes of plants and animals temporarily suppress the deteriorating effects of the second law. This is possible because living things are open systems; that is, they are capable of taking in energy from their surroundings in the form of food and sunlight, intelligently processing the energy, and eliminating waste products.[5] This intelligent processing of energy involves energy transformation, the formation of new cells, and the repair of damaged cells and cell membranes. (Think about the implications of this as it pertains to the quality of food we eat and the importance of a balanced diet.) The ability of the life processes to compensate for the deteriorating effects of the second law is dramatically confirmed by the sudden increase in the rate of deterioration of any living thing at the instant of death.

A close look at life processes reveals not only how amazing these processes are but also how well adapted they are to counteracting entropy. An excellent example is the formation of living cells within the human body.

In humans, red blood cells survive for approximately 120 days and then need to be replaced. To get an idea of the magnitude of this replacement process, note that a small drop of blood contains *5 million* red blood cells. The formation rate of white blood cells, which are crucial to our immune system, varies depending upon the need for infection control. All the cells in our skeletal bones are replaced over a period of about seven years. The complexity of all these regenerative processes taking place while the body maintains a fully functional system seems incredible. It also gives new meaning to the old adage "I'm not the same person I used to be!"

An analogy may help to show how the life processes compensate for the deteriorating influence of the second law. A skilled maintenance worker can temporarily suppress the deteriorating influence of the second law on your house. When interior or exterior paint oxidizes or begins to peel, the worker repaints; when roofing shingles become old, the worker gets rid of them and puts down new ones; when appliances malfunction, the worker repairs or replaces them. As a result of all these fixes, the house may appear to be the same as it was when first built.

But what happens when our analogous maintenance worker grows old? The worker begins to lose the energy required to keep up with all the house's maintenance needs, and so the house begins to show its age.

The same is true for the body. As amazing as cell replacement and other counter-entropic life processes are, they can only postpone the inevitable. In fact, damaged and dying cells are direct evidence of the effects of the second law. Furthermore, our life processes function at the expense of our surroundings; that is, we transform valuable chemical energy into less valuable thermal energy, which, along with our waste, contributes to the increase in entropy in our surroundings. Ultimately, the aging process is the result of a gradual deterioration of the life processes themselves. The body's ability to manufacture and repair healthy, high-quality bone, tissue, and red blood cells, and to manufacture disease-fighting white blood cells, eventually yields to the relentless deteriorating influence of the second law. Thus the entropy of the body gradually increases, making it weak and more susceptible to disease. Ultimately, whether by naturally increasing weakness or the result of disease, the body dies.

The iron law of entropy wins out in the end for living

things as well as for material objects. We thus see how pervasive the second law is to the physical realm of life. But is it bounded by the physical? Its often subtle yet profound influences appear to reach out somewhere well beyond— perhaps to our very souls.

4

The Entropy Analogy: How the Second Law Applies in Nonphysical Realms

Life begets life. Energy creates energy. It is by
spending oneself that we become rich.
—*Sarah Bernhardt (1844–1923)*

Reader's Digest carried a story written by Nancy
Sullivan Geng that not only tugs at your heart but also
makes you think about the human consequences of the
second law. The story is about a young girl named Lauri and
her sixth-grade teacher, Mrs. Lake.

Lauri lived in a depressing family environment. Her
father was an alcoholic, and more often than not, Lauri
would fall asleep listening to her father yelling, her mother
crying, and doors slamming. The children in the family
sometimes came in for neglect and abuse themselves.

One Christmas, for example, Lauri and her sister used
their baby-sitting money to buy their dad a shoeshine kit,
lovingly wrapping it and anticipating how it would please
him. When they gave it to him, they watched in stunned
silence as he threw the shoeshine kit across the room, breaking it into pieces.

The story focuses on a life-changing event that took
place in Lauri's life during a student conference near the
end of the year. Parents came to school at scheduled times
and met with their child and Mrs. Lake. Laurie knew her
parents would not be coming despite her teacher's phone
calls and a reminder letter. It's hard to imagine how Lauri

must have felt as she sat in the classroom watching each student being called by Mrs. Lake into the conference room, where they were warmly greeted by their parents.

When each conference was finished, the student left with his or her parents. At the end of all the conferences, Lauri was left sitting alone in the classroom. But the last conference was not over! Mrs. Lake opened the door and invited Lauri to come in.

The event that followed is best described by the story's author.

Embarrassed that her parents had not come, Lauri folded her hands and looked down at the linoleum. Moving her desk chair next to the downcast little girl, Mrs. Lake lifted Lauri's chin so she could make eye contact. "First of all," the teacher began, "I want you to know how much I love you."

Lauri lifted her eyes. In Mrs. Lake's face she saw things she'd rarely seen: compassion, empathy, tenderness.

"Second," the teacher continued, "you need to know it is not your fault that your parents are not here today."

Again Lauri looked into Mrs. Lake's face. No one had ever talked to her like this. No one.

"Third," she went on, "you deserve a conference whether your parents are here or not. You deserve to hear how well you are doing and how wonderful I think you are."

In the following minutes, Mrs. Lake held a conference just for Lauri. She showed Lauri her grades. She scanned Lauri's papers and projects, praising her efforts and affirming her strengths. She had even saved a stack of watercolors Lauri had painted.

Lauri didn't know exactly when, but at some point in that conference she heard the voice of hope in her heart. And somewhere a transformation started.

As tears welled in Lauri's eyes, Mrs. Lake's face became misty and hazy—except for her drop earrings of golden curls and ivory pearls. What were once irritating intruders in oyster shells had been transformed into things of beauty.

It was then that Lauri realized, for the first time in her life, that she was lovable.[1]

Nothing rubs my heart raw like the thought of a child's life being destroyed bit by bit, beaten down and broken by the selfish, cruel, vindictive acts of adults who should know better, who could do so much better. I have thought a lot about the Lauris of this world, the millions of children around the planet whose last threads of hope are continually fraying, with no visible pearls of redemption. And somehow it puts me in mind of another sort of deterioration—the kind we have been studying. The deterioration described by the second law.

It appears to me to be no great stretch to perceive a type of entropy operating within human dynamics, including social institutions and interpersonal relationships. Maybe, in such cases, it is not true entropy we are talking about, but it *is* something very much like it. Call it the "entropy analogy." Its existence was etched on the heart of the little girl in our story.

In this chapter we will look at three versions of the entropy analogy: social, relational, and ethical entropy. All this lays a foundation for understanding the most important version of the entropy analogy: spiritual entropy. We will begin getting to that in the next chapter.

Decline and Fall

Edward Gibbon wrote a famous work called *The History of the Decline and Fall of the Roman Empire* in which he described the dissolution of that great empire as inevitable due to its moral decadence. Oswald Spengler, in his book *The Decline of the West,* attempted to prove that all cultures pass through a life cycle of growth and decay comparable to the biological cycle of living organisms. Whether the ideas presented by these men have merit or not, their works focus on a truth we are all aware of if we have studied history at all: human institutions have a way of collapsing and vanishing with a puff of smoke. What's at work here is *social entropy.*

One might think of the creation of a viable social institution as representing an increased social order within the institution's domain of influence. In the sciences we know that it is possible to increase physical order (that is, to decrease physical entropy) within a particular physical domain by the intelligent use of energy. For example, the construction of a new automobile, the cleaning and rearranging of rooms, and the repair or replacement of skeletal bone cells within the human body all represent an increase in physical order within a given domain. These examples do not violate the second law, because the intelligent use of the energy required to locally increase order and decrease entropy in a given domain always causes a greater amount of disorder in the surroundings of that domain. This results in an increase in the total entropy of the universe. In our analogy, therefore, creating a new social institution designed to provide or promote some form of increased social order would not violate the entropy analogy.

Creating a successful social institution (with a resulting increase in order in that domain) is, however, no guarantee of its survival. Think about any social institution—a high school drama club, a parent-teacher organization, a city council, a state government, or a world empire. Its natural tendency to deteriorate is strikingly similar to the physical consequences of the second law. For deteriorate this institution will, unless it is continually infused with intelligently utilized energy, usually in the form of human effort and leadership.[2]

None of this is to suggest that social institutions are bad or that it is useless to create and seek to maintain them. They can be valuable, even crucial, during their period of existence. The point is to put their existence into perspective. A form of entropy is at work here just as surely as in the physical realm. Social institutions don't last. Nor do many interpersonal relationships.

Friendship Cooldown

In the mid-1950s I put in two years of active duty in the U.S. Army, most of it spent in what was then West Germany. Naturally, I formed some close friendships during that time. And when my army buddies and I went our separate ways, at the end of our tour of duty, we all agreed to stay in contact.

How did we do at fulfilling our promise? At first we did pretty well. Then, as our jobs got more demanding and our responsibilities as parents increased, our communication dropped to the exchange of Christmas cards once a year.

Several years ago, I determined with my wife to visit one of my army buddies—the one who had been my closest friend during those army days. We had not seen each other for nearly forty years. I contacted him to ask for the visit, and he welcomed it. Both of us felt an air of excitement as we looked forward to our reunion.

When we finally met, we had a great time reminiscing, over a long dinner, about the experiences and adventures we had shared nearly four decades earlier. We enjoyed catching up with what had gone on for us in the intervening years. But as we talked, it became clear to both of us that what had once been a high-quality, heartfelt relationship had degenerated into a mere acquaintance whose strongest remaining emotion was nostalgia.

I'm sure you recognize the kind of experience I had with my army buddy. We all realize that high-quality, empowering, vital personal relationships are hard to maintain over the long term. As in the physical realm, there is a natural cooling down. It's the effect of *relational entropy*.

Consider the role of forgiveness in maintaining long-term relationships. For such a relationship to flourish, both partners must be willing to ask for and freely grant forgiveness for the hurts that are bound to occur. Asking for and granting forgiveness takes considerable humility, patience, courage, and effort. When forgiveness is granted, the person being forgiven usually experiences a decrease in some combination of social, ethical, and moral entropy—depending, of course, on the particular hurt inflicted. This type of entropy often exposes itself in the form of guilt.

In any personal relationship—be it a friendship, a marriage, or some other family or social relationship—we must *intelligently* expend energy simply to keep relationships healthy and to repair the damage that invariably occurs. That way, while many relationships will go cool or even cold, we may be able to keep our most important relationships intact as long as our lives last.

Human Nature

The glorification of selfishness and rebellion. Senseless acts of sociopathic violence. Apathetic attitudes toward stealing, cheating, deception, and marital infidelity. Terrorism as a means for communicating outrage at perceived social injustice. Freeway murders. Eleven year olds without any remorse being tried as adults for murder. Doctors who kill their patients. Are these examples enough to convince you (if you needed convincing) that there is a natural tendency for the deterioration of ethical and moral values? More important than social and relational entropy, and often connected to them, is *ethical entropy.*

The ethical condition of a culture or a society is, in part, a reflection of the ethical character of its people and their leadership. And thus some oscillations in the ethical tone can exist as a result of changes in external conditions and individual attitudes. But ethical entropy is always at work, creating a bent toward wrongdoing in individual lives and in groups.

Today, absolute standards for behavior are being applied less and less frequently. For an increasing percentage of our society, everyone is doing what seems right in his or her own eyes.[3] Personal character, honor, and integrity are not considered as important in our present society as they were in years past. Instead, there is a widespread conception that an individual's personal life is of little consequence to his or her professional life. Our business and political landscape is littered with the entropy associated with such thinking.

When we think about it, each of us has a certain sense of right and wrong when it comes to behavior. To be sure, we will differ on the existence of some values, and we will disagree on just where to draw the line on others, but with respect to right or wrong behavior, we can expect to note more similarities than differences. C. S. Lewis, the well-known English author, suggested that a careful study would reveal that this similarity also extends back to the ancient Egyptians, Babylonians, Hindus, Chinese, Greeks, and Romans. Cowardice on the battlefield, double-crossing your friends, selfishness, and unfairness have never been admired.[4] Lewis refers to this general sense of right and wrong as the rule of decent behavior, or the law of human nature.[5]

What is unique about this particular law is that (unlike the physical laws, such as the first and second laws of thermodynamics or the law of gravity) the law of human nature tells us *what we ought to do,* not necessarily *what we do.* Therefore, this law could never be ascertained solely by external observations, that is, by observing our behavior. About this, Lewis said:

> There is one thing, and only one, in the whole universe which we know more about than we could learn from external observation. That one thing is Man. We do not merely observe men, we are men. In this case we have, so to speak, inside information; we are in the know. And because of that, we know that men find themselves under a moral law, which they did not make, and cannot quite forget even when they try, and which they know they ought to obey.[6]

It is this self-discernment dimension that makes the law of human nature uniquely human. Lewis considers, in some detail, a number of reasons for why this law of human nature is different from herd instincts or social conventions.[7]

Is it possible that many of the similarities that exist in the ethical and moral teachings of the world religions of Hinduism, Buddhism, Islam, Judaism, and Christianity are related in some way to this law of human nature? What lies behind this uniquely human law? Is it related to what we call "conscience"? If so, how did it get there? Is it purely a biological thing, or does it go beyond the biological? These questions deserve some exploration—and explore we will, for ethical entropy is closely connected to spiritual entropy.

Regardless of the provenance of ethical entropy, it is possible to locally reduce the amount of this type of entropy through the intelligent use of energy. For example, ethical entropy production could be reduced by the passage of strict laws, swiftly enforced. Remember, however, that the intelligent processing of energy in one domain will result in the generation of a greater amount of entropy in the surrounding domains. Thus, strict laws that are strictly and swiftly enforced may result in the loss of certain societal freedoms or, at the individual level, in miscarriages of justice. An increase in energy expended through teaching children and teens about the dangers of alcohol and drugs may save lives, which is commendable, but the surrounding domains of education will suffer a reduction in available time for teaching other subjects. Stricter laws and increased education, however, would not address the core of the problem: human nature—the reason we so often do not do what we know we ought to do.

Entropy and Freedom of Choice

Not many would disagree that as individuals we have a freedom of choice that embraces a wide scope of attitudinal and behavioral alternatives. But for the good of society, some choices are restricted or forbidden, and so we enact laws designed to direct our behavior. Even laws cannot stop the free exercise of choice, however, and because we have freedom of choice, each of us can directly or indirectly influence the amount of entropy we generate within our individual spheres of influence.

Consider two extreme examples: terrorists and Mother Teresa.

By an act of free choice, on September 11, 2001, nineteen terrorists hijacked four commercial airliners, laden with jet fuel and passengers, and intentionally flew two of them into the twin towers of the World Trade Center in New York and a third into the Pentagon in Washington. The fourth airliner crashed in Pennsylvania before reaching its intended target. This horrific tragedy killed around three thousand people. The terrorists' decision to attack in this way resulted in a devastating increase in entropy—not only physical entropy but also emotional and psychological entropy in the lives of the relatives and friends of the victims. Who can ever erase from their minds the pictures that emerged from New York and Washington both during and following the heinous attack?

At the other extreme, using her freedom of choice, Mother Teresa chose to reach out to the poor around the world—people who were living in chaotic circumstances and conditions. Beginning with her Pure Heart Home for Dying Destitutes in Calcutta, India, Teresa and her Missionaries of Charity (a religious order she founded) spread their good works to communities of the poor world-wide. Mother Teresa's decision to serve the poor brought some measure of order, stability, compassion, love, and even joy into numerous lives that, prior to their encounter with Mother Teresa, had known little of such experiences.

What a contrast! The terrorists' decisions left a devastating trail of disorder and chaos in the lives of those people within their chosen sphere of influence; Mother Teresa's decisions left an honorable trail of order and peace in the lives of those people within her chosen sphere of influence.

You and I can and do much to influence the amount of entropy generated within our respective spheres of influence. We need to ask ourselves, *Does my involvement in a relationship tend to bring order, peace, and love or to bring disorder, chaos, and fear?* Or to put it another way, what role do we play in each of our relationships—the terrorist or the missionary? While most of us probably fall somewhere between the two extremes, all of us, by our freedom of choice, influence the amount of entropy produced within our relationships. It is clear that Mrs. Lake (the teacher in the story at the head of this chapter) had willingly and with great conviction made her choice.

And with this reminder of ethical entropy, we come to a closely allied dimension of the entropy analogy: spiritual entropy. The second law of thermodynamics implies that there must be something beyond this physical universe we live in. There must, in fact, exist some transcendent spiritual realm.

5

Time Curve:
Why Entropy Implies a Beginning and an End for the Universe

It is better to know some of the questions than all of the answers.

—*James Thurber (1894–1961)*

Whan we are small children, it seems to us that the world has always been the way it is at that time. Daddy has always been a firefighter. Mommy has always wiped little kids' runny noses. Our family has always lived in the brick house with the porch swing. While we, as small children, are keenly aware of our own aging and growth (we love birthdays! we love it when grown-ups tell us how big we are getting!), we think the rest of the world is essentially constant. Only later do we discover the truth: everyone we know and everything we see is undergoing some type and rate of change. We have come on stage in the midst of an unfolding drama.

In something like the same way, cosmologists (those who study the history and makeup of the universe) have had to struggle with whether the universe has always existed and always will or whether it had a beginning in time and will have an ending. For years, many cosmologists promoted some type of the "steady state hypothesis," which claims that the universe has always existed pretty much as it is today—and that, as far as we can tell, it always will. That hypothesis seemed to provide a scenario within which natural laws could operate uniformly forever. But ironically, one particular natural law has largely overthrown the steady state hypothesis.

That law, of course, is the second law of thermodynamics. This fundamental law (in ways that we will shortly examine) clearly implies that the universe had a beginning in time and that it will also come to an end of some sort. Some cosmologists still propose variations on the steady state hypothesis in an attempt to keep it alive. But most now admit—sometimes begrudgingly, like a little child who is saddened to learn that his world is not as constant as he had thought—that we live in a universe that once was not and someday will again no longer be, at least in the form we know it today.

I believe that the reason some persons have been reluctant to give up the idea of an eternal physical universe is that it raises disturbing (to them) implications. It seems to suggest the possibility of a God—one who is greater than the universe, because he is eternal and it is not, and who perhaps created the universe and is capable of consummating its history. For naturalists, this is an unwelcome possibility and one that they deal with in a number of ways. But the truth of the second law and its time curve remains.

In this book we have so far been merely touring the front garden in our discussions of physical entropy and various nonphysical entropy analogies. With this consideration of the universe's origin and destiny, along with the unique negative quality this law possesses, we have arrived at last at the threshold of the book's main subject: spiritual entropy.

Uneven Energy

To scientists, the universe is an "isolated system," meaning that energy and matter can neither enter it nor leave it. At the same time, matter and energy are distributed unevenly within this system. Scientists describe this as the universe being in "disequilibrium." Thus, in the universe, we have a domain where entropy can act, and in fact is acting, in an inexorable way.

Let's take a closer look at disequilibrium, because it is the source of some important conclusions about the story entropy tells.

As an example of disequilibrium in the universe, the sun is much hotter than its surroundings in our solar system. Because of this difference in temperature, thermal energy is continually being transferred by solar radiation from the higher-temperature sun to the Earth as well as to the other planets in our solar system and to outer space, which are all at lower temperatures than the sun. This energy transfer, along with the energy transformation (believed to be nuclear fusion) responsible for the sun's high surface temperature, causes a continuing increase in the entropy of the universe. Such is the case for every star in every galaxy. The second law demands it.

If we focus our attention on the earth itself, we don't find much equilibrium here either. For instance, we humans, along with all warm-blooded birds and animals, are not in thermal equilibrium with our environment. Therefore, thermal energy is transferred from the warm creatures to the cooler environment. This energy transfer, along with the energy transformation from chemical energy in our food to thermal energy (in order to maintain body temperature), also causes an increase in entropy.[1]

In addition, and on a much larger scale, entropy is continually being generated by all the energy required to fuel the many different industries that drive our modern civilization. The list of such industries is all-encompassing: transportation, manufacturing, electric and gas utilities, communication, health care, construction, education, entertainment, and national defense. We live in an energy-intense world.

So, whether on a grand cosmic scale or simply in the

process of sustaining life, the second law requires that the entropy of the universe be continually increasing. In fact, if we construct a simple graph that pictures the entropy of the universe as a function of historical time, with entropy on the vertical axis and time on the horizontal axis, the entropy curve increases with time as shown in the accompanying figure. The recorded history segment of the curve is obviously not to scale. Also, the curve would not be smooth; it would have sudden jumps in entropy for catastrophic events, such as when stars exploded, volcanoes erupted, hurricanes came ashore, or wars broke out. But the general shape of the entropy-time curve exhibits a continually decreasing slope (degree of steepness) until the slope becomes zero—a horizontal line. The reason for this is also a consequence of the second law.

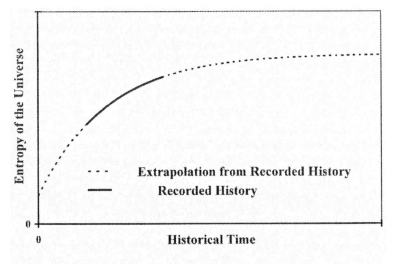

Entropy-Time Curve of the Universe

Here's why. The second law requires that whenever energy is transferred from one place to another (such as solar radiation) or transformed from one form to another form (such as nuclear to thermal) there is a decrease in available energy. The result is a decrease in the "driving potential" for future energy transfer or transformation, and so a decrease in the rate of entropy generation. When there is *no* available energy (no driving potential), there will be *no* entropy generation—zero slope.

As a small-scale example of this, a hot piece of metal cools when exposed to cooler air because of the transfer of thermal energy to the air. How fast this thermal energy transfer takes place is related to the difference between the temperature of the metal and that of the air, meaning that the driving potential for the rate of energy transfer is the temperature difference. As the metal's temperature decreases while it cools, so does the rate of energy transfer, resulting in a decrease in the rate of entropy generation. When the metal reaches the air temperature, the rate of energy transfer will go to zero, so will the rate of entropy generation.

But regardless of the steepness of the curve, it *is* a curve we are talking about and not a straight line, and this raises some important questions.

From Start to Finish

Since the shape of the entropy-time curve of the universe is dictated by the second law, we are forced to consider where the curve starts and where it ends. First, extending the curve back in time (shown by the dashed line to the left) implies that at some point in time the entropy of the universe would have been at a minimum value, or a point of minimum disorder (maximum order). This naturally raises the question of the origin of our space and time.

As an example of this idea, think about a car, let's say a Chevy Corvette. At what point in the life of that sports car would it have been in a state of minimum entropy, or maximum order? Probably when the Corvette rolled off the assembly line, spotless and with all of its sophisticated systems and subsystems able to function exactly as designed. Considerable creativity and intellect went into its design, and a large amount of energy was expended in its fabrication. The point of its minimum entropy, therefore, was when it had just been manufactured—its "origin."

For a new automobile, we not only know how all the order got there, but we also know the source of that order. But what about the universe at its point of origin? Where did all the order come from?

If the universe has not always existed and was incapable of creating itself, one logical conclusion is that a transcendent, intelligent Being—namely, God—created the universe for his own purposes. Science cannot provide absolute proof that a divine Creator exists, but its observations about the material world offer indirect evidence for his existence. The fact of a beginning for the universe, and the need to explain that beginning, is certainly one form of indirect evidence for God.

This subject is important—so important that it will be taken up in much greater detail in chapter eight. There we will look at the evidence for, and the implications of, intelligent design in the world. For now, it is sufficient to register the truth that an extension of the entropy-time curve to the past leads to a conclusion consistent with the existence of God.

Meanwhile, a second, and somewhat disturbing, question surfaces when we extend the entropy-time curve far into the future, as pictured in the figure by the dashed line to the right. What's disturbing is the recognition that in the absence of some outside intervention, our universe is heading toward a point in time where its entropy will be a maximum. That is, the universe's condition will be one of maximum disorder with no usable energy. Under such circumstances, no naturally occurring processes could take place. Life could not exist.

Sir James Jeans, one of the most famous astronomers during the first half of the twentieth century, wrote the following in response to this implication of the second law:

> Physics tells the same story as astronomy. For, independently of all astronomical considerations, the general physical principle known as the second law of thermodynamics predicts that there can be but one end to the universe—a "heat-death" in which the total energy of the universe is uniformly distributed, and all the substance of the universe is at the same temperature. This temperature will be so low as to make life impossible. It matters little by what particular road this final state is reached; all roads lead to Rome, and the end of the journey cannot be other than universal death.[2]

Jeremy Rifkin makes a similar observation, but he expresses it in terms of time:

> Time can only exist as long as there is available energy to perform work. The amount of real time expended is a direct reflection of the amount of energy used up. As the universe runs out of available energy, fewer and fewer occurrences can happen—which means less and less "real" time is still available. Eventually, as the final equilibrium state of heat death is reached, everything will stop occurring. Time, then, will no longer

exist as we experience it, because nothing will any longer be occurring.[3]

Is there any way to stop or delay this impending "ultimate chaos"? Is there any hope of some outside intervention before this heat death occurs?

This perplexing situation has caused scientists and philosophers considerable consternation ever since Clausius's articulation of the second law in 1865. In an attempt to escape the discomforting concept of the ultimate heat death of the universe, some scientists have suggested that the entropy-time curve of the universe might oscillate. In other words, if the total mass of the universe is great enough, the expansion of space might reverse itself and the universe would begin to retract. Then it would begin to expand all over again.[4] This could be considered a modern version of the steady state hypothesis, in that it implies the eternal existence of the universe.

The problem with the oscillation hypothesis, however, clever as it may be, is that it offers no verifiable mechanisms or substantiated evidence that it corresponds with reality.[5] Besides, astronomical observations are making it look more and more like the mass of the universe is not sufficient to cause the hypothesized universal retraction. In other words, scientifically speaking, it seems that the universe is going to keep expanding and that Sir James Jeans' prediction of heat death is accurate.

If science can foresee no alternative to heat death, do we have any other reason to hope for escape from the effects of entropy? In fact, we do, and as with the idea of a beginning to entropy, it points to a God who transcends the universe. But that exciting subject has to wait until this book's final chapter, coming after we have developed the context of physical entropy and spiritual entropy further.

Right now, we must consider a final way in which the

entropy-time curve of the universe—portraying, as it does, the inevitable progress toward disorder of the universe we live in—makes us ask questions about God.

The One Negative Law

The second law of thermodynamics is the only natural law that is negative. All other known natural laws are essentially neutral; that is, they are innately neither positive nor negative, neither good nor bad. But entropy is unique in that it describes disorder, degradation, deterioration, decay, and death.[6]

By way of contrast, let's consider the law of gravity. Gravity is neither good nor bad in itself. Our experiences with gravity determine how we view it. If it were not for gravity, we would not be able to walk, and, we would all be thrown off the surface of the earth by the centrifugal forces that result from the earth's rotation on its axis. These experiences with the law of gravity are positive and good. On the other hand, if we decide to jump down a stairwell or off the roof of a house, our experience with the law of gravity might not be so good. This would not be because gravity is bad but because, given the circumstances, our decision to jump was bad.

Unlike the law of gravity and other natural laws, the second law of thermodynamics is not neutral. In fact, it is far from neutral. Our experiences with the second law are overwhelmingly negative.

Sure, there are some experiences with the second law that, depending upon one's point of view, could be considered positive. For example, grass clippings and raked leaves decompose to become fertilizer for vegetable gardens and flower beds. Death eventually comes to the Stalins and Hitlers in our world, cutting off their grim trails of destruction. The entropy-generating processes of heat transfer, diffusion, and chemical reactions are integral parts of the life processes in living organisms. And in addition to these examples, no doubt there are other such experiences that, depending on our perspective, might be considered positive. We might also speculate that there could be some positive but obscure manifestations of the second law that we do not know about. But the fact still remains that the vast majority of our experiences with the second law are negative.

Entropy imposes itself in the form of limitations and in the natural tendency toward confusion and chaos, toward decay and destruction. Entropy is why ice cream melts and people die. It is why cars rust and forests burn. Preponderantly, the second law describes effects that we don't want to see.

Why, among all of the fundamental laws of nature, are our experiences with the second law so uniquely negative? Could it be because the second law is tied up with God and spiritual things? With this line of questioning, the door is opened to enter the realm of spiritual entropy. We first must consider why it matters that we uncover the truth in this area.

6

Truth Matters:
The Possibility of Arriving at Real
Knowledge of God

> Truth has no special time of its own. Its hour is
> now—always.
>
> —*Albert Schweitzer (1875–1965)*

Edward Smith was one of the most excited, enthusiastic men I have ever met.[1] And no wonder. When I met him, Edward had spent most of his spare time for the past ten years working on the design for a new type of gas turbine engine. This design was so full of potential that, if it worked, it would change gas turbine technology and would make Edward a wealthy man.

Having been a design engineer for a large company, Edward was a skilled draftsman. He had already made detailed drawings for every working part of his engine, including cutaways and assembly drawings. The results made him think he was really on to something.

When he had finally become convinced (several months before I met him) that everything would work, he had taken early retirement from his job. He did this knowing that he would need to devote all his time to applying for a patent and finding investment capital in order to build a prototype.

Edward was also seeking technical consultation for his patent application. That's where I came into the picture.

Several days after our first phone conversation, Edward appeared in my office. He was a stocky, well-built man with dark hair and a bright, cheerful smile. His enthusiasm for his work was, if anything, even more contagious in person than it had been over the phone. And his warm, pleasant personality was such that I immediately took a liking to him.

During our meeting, I told Edward that I wanted to do a preliminary overview of the thermodynamics of his engine before entering into any longer-term consulting arrangement. He agreed to this and gave me a set of drawings, along with a detailed description of the various thermal processes involved in the workings of the proposed engine.

I studied what he had given me for several days and was impressed with a number of his innovations. One particular innovation involved a clever way of enhancing the amount of turbine-blade cooling. This allowed for higher combustion gas temperatures, which in turn would increase engine efficiency. Another innovation involved a unique way of packaging the various engine components. This gave the engine a favorable horsepower-to-size ratio.

But there was something about the design that bothered me, something that just did not seem right. I could not put my finger on what it was.

I sat down one afternoon, turned off the phone in my study, and hunkered down over the plans to uncover the cause of my unease. Altogether, the sequence of processes Edward had built into the turbine cycle would provide efficiencies exceeding those of any known turbine engine design—efficiencies that were surely good enough to attract the attention of would-be investors. But still, something bothered me. I leaned over the stack of papers on my desk and dug, then dug some more.

It was *there*, in one of the subtle processes that made up the cycle. After a little analysis and a few calculations, I sat back in my chair, steepled my fingers, and stared down at the paper in front of me. The design would not work. It violated the second law. Although all of the other thermal processes involved were valid, the engine could *never* work.

Bad News

Edward Smith had poured his heart and soul into his design for ten years, spending every available hour at his work. I had been hired to help him make his dream a reality. And instead, I had just discovered that his dream did not have a *chance* for success, like a stalk of nearly ripened wheat broken off by a sudden gust of wind. I stared at the detailed drawings before me—the thin crisp lines, meticulous circles, the tiny letters, and the carefully inserted dimensions. All of this effort was doomed to futility before the first prototype part could be machined, before the first investor could be found. How could I break the bad news to Edward?

At first I didn't. I procrastinated. Instead of making a phone call to set up a meeting, I went over the drawings and thermal process descriptions again. And again and again, for nearly a week. Each time I was hoping to find an error in my analysis of that one culprit thermal process. But I could not.

Finally, in good conscience, I could delay no longer. I called Edward to set up a meeting. In our short conversation, without going into any detail, but to at least give him some warning, I hinted that I had found a potential problem.

Two days later, Edward was back in my office, his face still filled with the engaging enthusiasm I had seen earlier. After all, Edward had encountered and solved many problems during the ten years he had been designing his engine. From his perspective, if I had discovered a problem, this would simply be one more hurdle for him to overcome.

But I knew differently. I knew it was much more than that. I knew that the issue I had discovered in Edward's design was an issue that could never be solved.

I tried to break the news as gently as possible. I started slowly and circled incrementally toward the problem, alluding to the invariability of physical laws and then, ever so carefully, to the second law. As the seriousness of my words began to sink in, Edward's confident attitude and enthusiasm began to fade.

It was one of the most difficult things I have ever had to do. I felt like a medical doctor sharing a verdict of terminal illness with a patient. I even encouraged Edward to get a second opinion.

I will never forget Edward's response. After the initial shock over what I had told him had subsided, he told me that he remembered hearing about the second law of thermodynamics when he was in college. He said he had not understood it very well at the time and afterward had never made an effort to understand it any better. In fact, he acknowledged that he had not given the second law *any* consideration as he was deciding on the various thermal processes involved in his turbine engine.

What a tragedy! The second law was there, whether Edward took account of it or not. I can't help thinking that since then he has never ignored entropy again. At least I hope so.

For my part, the lesson I took away from the experience was this: truth matters! In this chapter we will be exploring whether one can know truth in matters of science or spirituality. Most importantly, can we really know that God exists?

Proof and Reality

Edward Smith was crushed by the news I had to give him. Any of us would be if we were in his spot—no one wants to be deceived about what we think to be true. And therefore it is natural for us to desire proof that something is true before we buy into it. Unfortunately, many fundamental concepts we encounter in life, though they may be true, cannot be proved to be true in an absolute sense. The existence of God is one of those fundamental concepts.

What most people do not recognize is that *all* fundamental principles of science fall into the same category, including the first and second laws of thermodynamics. These two laws are called "theories" or "theoretical models." Scientists often use the term "model" because it suggest inexactness. A theoretical model, then, represents an approximation to reality. Some theoretical models are excellent approximations to reality. Others are not so good. Some are poor approximations to reality but represent the best explanation we have based on present knowledge.

Within the domain of theoretical models, scientists distinguish the fundamental from the secondary. Fundamental theoretical models are often referred to as "laws" or "principles," and these include the first and second laws of thermodynamics.[2] Both of these laws are considered to be excellent approximations to reality, because no one has found a naturally occurring exception to either law that has been scientifically substantiated.

Secondary models may be explained by logical reasoning in terms of the fundamental laws upon which they depend. Fundamental laws, however, do not depend upon any other laws. Science has no means for explaining why a fundamental law exists; neither can science prove its validity in an absolute sense.

Although it cannot be proved in an absolute sense, the validity of fundamental laws can be tested or verified by experimental observation. In the case of the first and second laws of thermodynamics, as I have said, no valid experimental data has ever been shown that would question their scientific integrity. Thus, while these two laws have never and can never be proved in an absolute sense, you would be hard pressed to find a scientist or engineer who did not believe in their reality.

Perhaps this idea can be made clearer by considering the humble snowflake. Growing up, you probably heard that no two snowflakes are exactly the same. And that's a true statement—as far as anyone knows. But to prove this hypothesis in an absolute sense would require a study of every snowflake that has ever existed in the past, every snowflake that is falling anywhere in the world today, and every snowflake that could ever exist in the future. This, obviously, is an impossible task. After many studies conducted over many years, however, no one has ever observed two identical snowflakes. This gives considerable credibility to the uniqueness-of-snowflakes hypothesis. Although there is no absolute proof in the matter, scientists have no hesitation in believing in the uniqueness of snowflakes.

The analogy with the laws of thermodynamics is clear enough, isn't it? Hold on. There's more.

Besides the fact that the first and second laws cannot be proved in any absolute sense, the scientific community had to overcome an additional obstacle in accepting the reality of these laws. Remember that thermodynamics is the study of energy. And remember that energy is invisible. It thus cannot be observed or measured directly—it is an abstract concept that can only be measured indirectly. For example, we know that an automobile traveling at seventy miles an hour has kinetic energy because we have seen what that kinetic energy can do to lives and property when the automobile crashes. Also, we know that gasoline has chemical energy because we have seen what happens when a lighted match is tossed into an open pan of gasoline. (I don't recommend that you try it—the sudden transformation of energy can be quite dramatic!)

But despite the invisibility of energy, no one doubts that it exists. Thus this obstacle is not an insurmountable one. It is not necessary that something be directly measurable or observable in order for it to exist and to be recognized as reality. The great body of knowledge known as the science of thermodynamics, along with the vast assortment of processes, devices, and systems surrounding us that were engineered from its understanding, provide ample testimonies to this fact.

We can study the first and second laws in textbooks and classrooms. And we can accept their reality despite the fact that we cannot prove them in an absolute sense nor see them with our eyes nor even explain why they exist. We accept the reality of these two laws because of reasoned study, including confirming experimental observations, and because no one has ever been able to disprove either of them.

And so that brings us to the question I want to plant in your mind: Might there be an analogy here between the reality of the first and second laws and the reality of God?

Spiritual Fundamentals

It is unreasonable to reject the validity of the existence of the first and second laws merely because they cannot be proved in an absolute sense. Can one make a reasonable determination regarding the existence of the God and Christ of the Bible merely on the basis that their existence cannot be proven in an absolute sense?[3] Or, as with the first and second laws, can the God and Christ of the Bible be indirectly tested by experiential observation?[4] That is, can the hypothesis of God be considered verifiable not with the use of high-tech scientific instrumentation but by careful observation and reason?

In the book of Jeremiah one reads, "If you search with all your heart, I will let you find me, says the Lord."[5] This verse is appealing to me, as a scientist and engineer, because it appears to be an invitation for an experiment—one that is open to anyone who is willing to search for the truth of the matter. Of course, this invitation sets forth some conditions for the search to be successful. We have to search for the real God and not settle for imitations; we have to search with all our heart; and so on. But then, for any legitimate *scientific* research to be successful, the methods and instruments used must be appropriate to, and calibrated for, the specific physical phenomena being investigated.

What is most interesting to me is that the biblical invitation strongly suggests that God wants us to find him—that he wants us to verify the reality of his existence. And over the centuries, countless numbers of men and women have taken him up on his invitation and in fact *have* found him, coming to a conviction about the reality of the God and Christ of the Bible. Many were, and—even in our day—many continue to be, willing to lose everything, even their lives, rather than to deny the validity of their findings. Instead of discounting their conviction as some kind of religious fanaticism, we might consider their accumulation of experience as evidence that the invitation—and the issuer of the invitation—are for real.

In our day, however, many people have latched on to the idea that nothing is true in all places at all times for all people. They say that truth, especially if it is in any way related to morality or religion, is strictly dependent on the situation or the people involved. This philosophy is known as relativism. For relativists, the thought of searching for a single God who created everything and rules all is nonsense.

To expose some potential dangers of this paradigm about truth, consider the following questions about the second law of thermodynamics:

- Is the second law a reality, or is it imaginary?
- Do inaccuracies in our description of the second law invalidate the reality of the law?
- Does the existence of the second law in any way depend upon what you or I think or know about it?
- If you or I do not believe in the second law, or if we have never heard about it, does our disbelief or lack of

knowledge have any effect on its existence?
- Does our disbelief or lack of knowledge have any effect on the implications that the second law's existence has for our lives?[6]

Reason demands that the reality of the second law's existence, and the truth of its implications for our lives, are the same for everyone. Also, the second law's existence and implications are totally independent of our belief, understanding, or interest in it. It would be logical to assume that if our personal understanding of the second law is limited or flawed in some way, then decisions we make based upon that understanding will likely also be limited or flawed.

Now, in an analogous manner, consider the following similar questions pertaining to the existence of God:

- Is God a reality, or is he imaginary?
- Do inaccuracies in our description of God invalidate the reality of God?
- Does the existence of God in any way depend upon what you or I think or know about him?
- If you or I do not believe in God, or if we have never heard about him, does our disbelief or lack of knowledge have any effect on his existence?
- Does our disbelief or lack of knowledge have any effect on the implications that God's existence has for our lives?

In our society, some people view faith as nothing more than a personal preference. They express their view something like this: "If believing in God is meaningful to you, then for you he exists; if it is not meaningful to me, then for me he doesn't exist." Consider the irrationality of such a view. This kind of reasoning implies that our *preference* can have an influence on the existence or nonexistence of God.

Our preference quite possibly would be that God not exist, since that would leave us free of any type of accountability to him. In the same vein, our preference would surely be that the second law not exist, since it imposes such negative limitations. But it *does* exist.

Again, it is only logical that if our personal understanding of God is limited or flawed in some way, then decisions we make based upon that understanding will likely also be limited or flawed. You have probably heard the saying "Truth matters and ultimate truth matters ultimately." That saying is so, well, true.

For those who wear the label Relativist proudly, I would appeal to their reason and suggest that they reconsider the possibility that absolute truth, at least in some areas, may actually exist and in particular that a God who wants them to know him may actually exist. Ultimate truth matters ultimately.

This chapter began with the true story of Edward Smith, who devoted ten years of his life to working on an invention that did not have a chance for success because he chose to ignore the second law. As tragic as that experience was for Edward, think for a moment about the greater tragedy of a person who has lived his or her entire life uninformed about, or simply choosing to ignore, the existence of God and the implications that his existence carries, if in fact, God is a reality.

The potential for this greater tragedy is never far from my conscious thought, probably because I cannot forget another experience. This experience took place at the bedside of a dying man who had suddenly found himself in the grips of such a tragedy—his own.

Attitude Adjustment, Courtesy of Death

John, a good friend of mine, asked me one day if I would visit his father, Phil, who was lying in a local hospital.[7] Phil was dying of cancer, and he had asked his son if he knew of anyone who was familiar with the Bible and who might be willing to talk with him. John came to me, and of course I agreed to go.

When I went to the hospital a couple of days later, I took another friend along with me. After we introduced ourselves to the sick man, Phil began to tell us a little about his life, how he grew up in Georgia, coming to Detroit during World War II because good jobs were plentiful. He shared with us his experiences in finding a job, getting married, buying a home, raising his family, helping his kids through college, and in recent years, enjoying his grandchildren.

Now suddenly, with no real warning, Phil found that he had terminal cancer, leaving him only a short time to live. As he lay alone in his hospital bed, facing imminent death, he had come to the realization that he had lived his entire adult life ignoring the implications of there being a God. He related that he had had an introduction to the God of the Bible as a young boy in Georgia. But he had chosen, as an adult, not to pursue the subject any further when he moved to Detroit. It was a decision for which he now expressed considerable regret.

Phil said that, because of the choice he had made, neither his children nor his grandchildren had had any encouragement from him to even consider the possibility of the reality of God. He had set the example for his family, and they were following it, living their lives apart from an interest in God. Now, forty-five years too late, he recognized the tragedy of his decision.

About to experience personally the reality of death, Phil had many unanswered questions—serious questions. Questions about God, about death, about life after death, about heaven and hell. He expressed great concern about whether he had unfulfilled obligations to God. All of these issues involved questions he had been too "busy" all of his adult life to wrestle with or seek answers to. These questions and concerns now loomed with such importance as to make most of the things he had spent his life doing pale into insignificance. Phil wept tears of regret that afternoon as he shared with us the anguish of looking back at all of the lost opportunities.

He died that same week.

Although none of us likes to think about it, we all, like Phil, will one day find ourselves staring into the face of death. The second law guarantees it. When that happens, what will we be thinking about? What will seem important? With what kinds of questions will we be wrestling?

If God is not a reality, it will not matter. But if he is?

I believe that the God of the Bible *is* real and that he imposed the uniquely negative law of entropy precisely because of the human tendency to go our own way without him. Let me share the basis I have for believing this.

7

The Curse:
An Exploration of Why and How Entropy
Came to Be

> Truth *happens* to an idea. It *becomes* true, is *made*
> true by events. Its verity *is* in fact an event, a
> process: the process namely of its verifying itself,
> its veri-*fication*. Its validity is the process of its
> validation.
>
> —*William James (1842–1910)*

A mother, with the best intentions, bought as her son's first pair of sneakers the kind that light up when the child steps. At first, the boy was delighted with his fun shoes. He loved to look down at his feet when walking around. Putting on his shoes never failed to cheer him up if something had made him upset. (Maybe more grown-ups would be happy if *we* wore light-up shoes.) But unfortunately, the battery power lighting up the boy's sneakers eventually ran down.

No longer when the boy ran across a room would his shoes flash red lights, attracting attention to him. The boy took his shoes off and pounded them against a step. But no red light shone. Since the shoes were not designed to allow the batteries to be replaced, the mother was helpless to provide an immediate solution that would make her heartbroken son stop crying. Though the boy was incapable of pronouncing the word "entropy," he had had one of his first conscious encounters with the negativity of the second law.

As we saw in chapter five, the second law of thermo-dynamics—uniquely among natural laws—is not neutral but predominately negative, producing disorder, deterioration, and death. The failure of battery power in a boy's shoes is among the least of the law's negative effects. In our pursuit of the truth about spiritual entropy, we must investigate the source of this negativity.

Because the second law of thermodynamics is a funda-mental law, science is unable to answer the question of *why* our experiences with the second law are so uniquely nega-tive.[1] If the answer does not lie in the realm of science, then where should we look? Perhaps theology has an answer.

Entropy—the Price of Rebellion

I have no way of knowing what paradigm about the Bible you may hold, whether you consider it to be a collec-tion of myths or the very Word of God or something in between. In a future chapter I will explain why I have deep respect for this theological sourcebook. But for now, let me merely point out that we should be able to agree that the Bible has had a tremendous influence on humanity for millennia and that it continues to have such an influence. That gives it a claim on our attention in any theological investigation. And in terms of what we are considering now, I can assure you that the Bible does contribute some inter-esting insights into the negativity question.

The Bible's position is that there is a God of the universe and in fact that he brought the universe into being. He is the Creator of all things, without exception. The first two chap-ters of the biblical book of Genesis present in general terms an account of God's creation of the universe, including the Earth and humankind. Our purpose for looking at the Genesis account here is not to consider the mechanisms God might have used in the process of Creation, nor the timing by which it all occurred, but rather to see what insight into the negativity question the Bible might contain.

In the Genesis account, a certain phrase appears over and over when God looks at what he has done. That phrase is "and God saw that it was good."[2] In fact, after the origin of man and woman (who are said to have been made in God's image), the Bible says, "God saw all that he had made, and it was *very* good."[3] In other words, God pronounced his approval of the entire creation and especially of humanity. But that approval begs an important question.

If the second law of thermodynamics, which has such a negative influence on the universe in general and on our lives in particular, was a part of the original creation, how could God, in good conscience, have looked upon what he had made and have said so emphatically that it was good? Several possibilities exist.

First, the possibility exists that God is a liar. I think we can dismiss this one immediately. A God who lies would seem to be a contradiction in terms. Furthermore, there is not a hint of evidence anywhere in the Bible to support the idea that God is a liar.

Second, it may be that God and I do not see eye to eye on the meaning of the word "good." This, I must admit, is a distinct possibility. In fact, I am sure there are a great many things on which God and I do not see eye to eye; otherwise, God would not be God. However, I know of no statement in the Bible that would suggest that God views the second law as good. For example, the Bible portrays human death—that most poignant effect of entropy—as a negative.

This leaves the third possibility, and that is that the second law, as we know it, did not exist at the time God pronounced creation to be "very good." To me, this seems to be the strongest possibility. We will have to explore it further, and our exploration begins with a question.

If the second law, as we know it, was not a part of the

original creation, then it had to have been imposed in the form we know it at some later time. Is there any evidence to support this idea?

The third chapter of Genesis gives an account of when the first man and woman, exercising their freedom of choice, rebelled against the authority of God.[4] It is immediately after the account of this rebellion that we begin to see the beginning of deterioration, or entropy. Listen to a part of what God said to the man as a consequence of his rebellion:

> Cursed is the ground because of you;
>> through painful toil you will eat of it
>> all the days of your life.
> It will produce thorns and thistles for you,
>> and you will eat the plants of the field.
> By the sweat of your brow
>> you will eat your food
> until you return to the ground,
>> since from it you were taken;
> for dust you are
>> and to dust you will return.[5]

Notice the use of words and phrases like "cursed," "painful toil," "sweat of your brow," and "to dust you will return" in the description of the consequences of humanity's rebellion. These same negative-sounding words could be used to describe the second law or at least some of its attendant negativity.

There is also a striking reference to the second law of thermodynamics in the New Testament. It is found in the eighth chapter of the book of Romans: "The creation was subjected to frustration, not by its own choice, but by the will of the one who subjected it, in hope that the creation itself will be liberated from its bondage to decay and brought into the glorious freedom of the children of God."[6] This seems to be a clear reference to, and confirmation of, what we have been considering. The words "frustration" and "bondage to decay" are accurate descriptions of the second law or at least some of its attendant negativity. Notice also the clear indication that an existing creation was subjected to this frustration and bondage to decay not by its own choice but by the will of the one who subjected it. This seems to suggest that it was God who imposed the negativity.

The implications are quite clear. First, the Bible is not ignorant of the pattern of behavior we call the second law of thermodynamics.[7] Second, if the biblical account is true, then the uniqueness of the second law among all the other fundamental laws of nature is not without reason. Unlike other natural laws, it was not, at least as we presently know it, a part of the original creation. Instead, it was imposed by God on the existing creation, as a curse, as a consequence of humankind's rebellion against God—what the Bible commonly calls "sin."[8] Perhaps the second law, in the form we know it, was imposed to continually remind us of the reality and negative consequences of sin.[9]

Imposing *Of* or Imposing *On?*

If the biblical account of God's response to Adam and Eve's rebellion describes what really happened, then living things in general, and humankind in particular, underwent a significant change at that point in history. The picture painted by words like "cursed," "painful toil," "sweat of your brow," "to dust you will return," "frustration," and "bondage to decay" is one that is dramatically negative—what we are talking about really was a curse. But naturally, we want to know how this curse worked. We might pose it as a question like this: Was the curse the imposition *of* the second law itself, with all of its attendant negativity, or was the curse imposed *on* an existing second law of thermodynamics, dramatically increasing its attendant negativity?

Obviously, with the exception of the One who imposed entropy, no one can really know which of the above two suppositions best represents what actually happened. And if we are honest about what we *don't* know, the truth may not be reflected by either of the suppositions above. However, let's consider three generalizations we *do* know to be true:

1. Science has clearly established the physical reality of the second law, along with the concept of entropy and its attendant negativity, as it exists today.
2. Our collective personal experiences and observations strongly suggest the existence of an entropy analogy, describing social, relational, ethical, and spiritual entropy and their attendant negativity.[10]
3. According to the Bible, a curse, with its attendant negativity, was imposed on an existing creation.

Our goal here is to try to determine whether the above two suppositions harmonize with these three known generalizations and whether they are subject to logical objections.

The first supposition—the curse being the imposition *of* the second law itself— harmonizes with the three known generalizations. But in doing so, it raises some issues that need to be addressed.

For example, as we presently understand them, such natural processes as heat transfer, mass diffusion, and chemical reactions are unidirectional or irreversible. That is, thermal energy in the form of heat always flows from the higher temperature to the lower, mass diffusion always flows from the higher concentration to the lower, and chemical reactions always take place from the higher energy states to the lower. The direction of these irreversible natural processes is presently governed by the second law, and they all produce entropy.

These processes are integral parts of the biochemical

and biophysical mechanisms of life today, and it seems reasonable that they must have been integral to the life that existed prior to the curse. It is impossible to imagine the world operating without these mechanisms, yet that is just what the first supposition requires. To put it in practical terms, if the second law did not exist in any form prior to the curse, how did solar energy from the sun warm the earth? How did the plants grow? How did animals and humans digest the food they ate? There is no answer to these questions if you accept the first supposition.[11]

In summary, it seems impossible to imagine that the second law of thermodynamics did not exist at all prior to the curse. We must reject the first supposition, even though it agrees with our three generalizations, because it has too many other problems attached to it.

The *second* supposition—the idea that the curse was imposed *on* an existing second law—also harmonizes with the three generalizations. Or rather, it harmonizes with them as long as one assumes that the entropy analogy, giving rise to social, relational, ethical, and spiritual entropy (with their attendant negativity), was a part of the curse but not of the original form of the second law. This seems quite reasonable, given the cause for which the curse was imposed. However, the idea that the curse was imposed on an existing second law raises some different issues. The most important issue relates to aging and death.

For humankind, aging and death represent the ultimate negativity. In terms of this second supposition, the curse was imposed on an existing second law, and thus on life that existed prior to the curse. The issue being raised here is this: before the imposition of the curse, how could living things have avoided aging and death while being under the influence of an existing second law? Remarkably, science may suggest an answer to this question. But first, some background is in order.

We know from our earlier discussion of living things (chapter three) that, at the present time, the life processes temporarily hold back the detrimental effects of the second law on living things. This is possible because the life processes are capable of repairing damaged cells and manufacturing new cells to replace dying cells. Aging and death take place because the life processes themselves eventually yield to the relentless deteriorating effects of the second law.

What could have prohibited aging and death in living things prior to the curse? The life processes would have that capability *if* the life processes themselves were in some way uniquely protected from the detrimental effects of the second law. Part of the curse could have been God's withdrawing this unique protection from the life processes, resulting in less than perfect cell repair and replacement, thus initiating the ultimate negativity of aging and death.

Some insight into this possible protection for the life processes may have been uncovered as a result of recent scientific efforts to unlock the secrets of the human genome—the complete set of human genes, containing about 750 megabytes of detailed digital information. The human genome comes packaged in twenty-three separate pairs of chromosomes. Virtually every cell has two complete sets of the human genome in its nucleus. Therefore, every time a new cell is manufactured or repaired, the required chromosomes for the cell would have to be "photocopied" from a similar cell. Because of the large number of repeated "photocopyings" required during a lifetime, some parts of the detailed biological information coded on the chromosomes can be lost or become blurred (loss of information represents an increase in entropy). The result? The aging of cells, and therefore the aging of organs and bodies.[12]

It is significant that this loss of information due to "photocopying" does *not* happen to egg cells or sperm cells.

The reason is the existence of a unique little biochemical machine called *telomerase.* Telomerase appears to make certain cells immortal.[13] Perhaps telomerase or some equivalent was present in *all* cells of living things prior to the curse and, at the time of the curse, God withdrew them.[14]

In light of the above, including the research into telomerase, it seems possible that the curse aspects of entropy were imposed *on* an existing form of the second law at the time of Adam and Eve's rebellion against God. We cannot fully know what that imposition entailed. Nor can we fully know what life was like before the imposition of the curse. But this supposition accords well with the biblical data and appears reasonable from a scientific standpoint as well.

Indirect Evidence

A world without the second law and its attendant negativity is difficult for us to imagine. We are beings who have lived with entropy all our lives and know no other existence. Yet if the above discussion tells us anything, it tell us that it *is* possible for us to speculate reasonably about the disordering effects of entropy and of the entropy analogy being imposed at a point following the origin of the universe. The imposition of entropy upon a preexisting form of the second law as a consequence of rebellion against God (and perhaps also to continually remind us of the negative effects of sin) makes sense. Thus, where science can offer no reason for the unique negativity of the second law, the Bible provides an explanation.

There is, in a sense, a mirror image to our discussion of the pre-entropic environment that existed before human sin entered the world, and that is the possibility that the curse of entropy may one day in the future be lifted. The Bible treats this eventuality just as matter-of-factly as it describes the primeval world that existed before entropy. The future entropy-free environment requires us to speculate again about what that sort of existence would be like, but that is an even more exciting activity than what we have been engaged in, for the future nonentropic state is one that the Bible says we can hope to participate in. We will get to this subject at the appropriate time, in the final chapter of this book.

For now, we can take note that the Bible offers a reasonable scenario for the attendant negativity of the second law of thermodynamics, including the different dimensions of the entropy analogy. We thus are closer to understanding spiritual entropy and have additional indirect evidence for the existence of God. In the following chapter we will look at more indirect evidence for God, not from speculations about the way the world was before the curse, but from investigations of the way the world is today. We are being perfectly reasonable when we believe that a God exists who created the world (and us) and who imposed on our race the effects of spiritual entropy.

8

Designer World: The Makeup of Reality and the Reality of God

> Earth's crammed with heaven,
> And every common bush afire with God;
> But only he who sees takes off his shoes,
> The rest sit round it and pluck blackberries.
> —*Elizabeth Barrett Browning (1806–61)*

A theist and an atheist were sitting side by side, both enjoying a sunset. (I know this sounds like the setup of a joke, but really it is quite serious.) The theist said, "How great is God! His canvas is as big as the sky. His palette is made up of every shade of color that exists. Of course, he must be powerful to be able to create such a scene, but he is obviously also a creative God to produce such beauty and a loving God to do it so that we can see it. And you know, I get a sense of peace from him, too, as this fiery spectacle calms down into twilight blues. How much I thank God for his goodness to us!"

"It *is* beautiful," agreed the atheist. "But 'God' has nothing to do with it. What we're seeing is water vapor on the horizon being understruck by the late-day sunlight and reflecting colors from the orange and red portions of the spectrum. The air beyond reflects blue like normal, until no more light strikes it and we see the blackness of infinite space beyond. If you want to thank something, thank evolution, which gave us such sensitive eyes. We have these eyes so that we can watch for predators and find food, but if they help us enjoy beauty, that's an added bonus for us. It's just a sunset; don't make too much of it."

One sunset, two very different perspectives.

We learned earlier that the entropy-time curve shows that the universe has not always existed, begging the question of whether there was an intelligence of some kind behind the creation of the universe.[1] Now it is time to explore in more detail the evidence for the Creator in the world. As usual, thermodynamics is our helper.

Argument from Design

It may be difficult for us to appreciate what went into the discovery of the two laws of thermodynamics. The existence of the first law was not recognized until 1850. Its recognition developed from the collective results of scientific experimentation involving many different scientists over a period of half a century.[2] The same was true for the second law. It took over forty years from the time it was initially perceived before it was fully articulated in 1865.[3]

The major reason that the first and second laws were effectively hidden from scientists' understanding until such a short time ago is that these laws are inextricably involved with energy, which is an abstract concept. Energy itself cannot be seen, nor can it be directly observed or measured. Energy's existence can be known only by its effects.

Fortunately, these effects can be observed and measured. For example, if thermal energy is transferred from a gas flame to water in a pan, it causes the temperature of the water to increase. Even though it is not possible to directly observe the thermal energy transferred from the gas flame to the water, we know the transfer takes place, because the water's temperature increase can be measured with a thermometer.

Besides warming water, energy makes light bulbs glow and cars accelerate. It warms our homes in the winter and cools them in the summer. It sustains life in living things, powers our appliances and runs our computers. We cannot doubt energy's reality or existence simply because we have never seen it. It is enough that we have seen its many effects for us to be confident of its existence.

But what about the reality of God? Can the reality of God's existence be "tested" in any way similar to that of the first and second laws of thermodynamics?

Dr. Ravi Zacharias discussed the significance of this question in his book *A Shattered Visage.*

> Several years ago, Encyclopedia Britannica published a 55-volume series entitled *The Great Books of the Western World.* Mortimer Adler, a noted philosopher and legal scholar, was co-editor of this series, which marshals the eminent thinkers of the western world and their writings on the most important ideas that have been studied and investigated over the centuries. ... These ideas are assembled for comparison and contrast. Very striking to the observant reader is that the longest essay is on God. When Mr. Adler was asked by a reviewer why this theme merited such protracted coverage, his answer was uncompromising. "It is because," he said, "more consequences for life follow from that one issue than from any other." ...
>
> It is not surprising, therefore, that Stephen Hawking concluded his most recent book, *A Brief History of Time,* asserting this to be the most significant factor in the human equation. Hawking, who holds Newton's chair as Lucasian professor of Mathematics

at Cambridge University, brilliantly laid out his view of the universe and ended with a humble assertion: the one question in need of an answer is the question of God. Science, with all of its strident gains, must still remain contented to describe the "what" of human observations. Only God can answer the "why."[4]

Seeking to know the reality of God's existence, as Mortimer Adler and Stephen Hawking underline, is in fact a very important pursuit. And just as we cannot see energy but only its effects, so we cannot see God but we can see what he has done. One big part of that is seeing what he has done in the world. This is a classical line of reasoning known in theology as the *argument from design.*

The argument from design has perhaps never been more popular than it is today. In fact, a group of respected, present-day scientists make up something called the "intelligent design movement" ("ID," for short). The faith commitments of ID scientists range from devout Christianity to agnosticism, but all of them share the belief that the scientific evidence points to some kind of intelligence behind the makeup and operation of the universe.[5]

The weight of evidence for design seems to grow as science, with its continually improving technology and instrumentation, probes deeper and deeper into nature's secrets. Recall the little biomolecular machine called *telomerase?* It has the capability of prohibiting the loss of information associated with repeated "photocopying" of DNA information for egg and sperm cells. In addition to telomerase, science has discovered that many cellular tasks required to sustain life are carried out by a variety of these biomolecular machines. Many of these machines are *irreducibly complex*—that is, each such machine requires a number of closely matched components *before* the machine could perform its function.[6] If any of its components are missing, the machine will not function. It seems impossible, then, that such machines could have evolved by chance from simpler forms through a process of natural selection. Therefore, they must have been designed that way.

The evidence for design is not limited to living things. For instance, there is the makeup of matter, including the variety and complexity of atomic and molecular structures. Think about the common water molecule, for example. It has properties that make it essential to living things. Water has the unusual behavior that when it freezes, its density decreases. This is what makes ice float—a characteristic important to the survival of aquatic life in the freshwater lakes that experience long, cold winters. These same water molecules have built-in molecular characteristics so that under the right conditions, crystallization in the form of snowflakes takes place, in which each snowflake has a symmetrical pattern of beauty that is uniquely its own. In other words, life as we know it could not exist without water. And water is just one such example. Scientists have identified dozens or even hundreds of "just right" characteristics on our planet without which life as we know it could not exist. Is it really reasonable to suppose that all these characteristics exist on earth by accident?

Design appears all around us. Rational thinking requires that serious consideration be given to the cause of this apparent design.

Thermodynamics as Evidence

In addition to all of the usual arguments about evidence for design in the world, I would like to promote one more. This evidence lies within thermodynamics itself.

The second law requires that all naturally occurring processes result in an increase in the entropy, or disorder, of the universe. Although it is possible to decrease the entropy, or increase order, within a particular local domain, it can *only* be done with "intelligence" and the utilization of energy. Energy alone cannot do it.

Intelligence can be actively involved in the process, as with the skilled maintenance worker who carefully repairs and replaces whatever is necessary to maintain a house. Or it can precede the process. In other words, the intelligence can go into the design of the system, which then has the appearance of intelligence. In engineering we refer to this designed-in intelligence as "artificial intelligence" or "smart systems." Examples of this in nature could be things like the life processes in living things or the molecular structures responsible for crystallization.

The concept, therefore, that the mechanism of unintelligent chance could bring order and even the appearance of design out of disorder, and could bring the complex organism from the simple, not only appears to be irrational and illogical but also appears to contradict much of what science knows about living organisms and the second law.

Consider the highly ordered genetic code compressed into a human DNA molecule—750 megabytes of uniquely sequenced digitized information. Although the size of the genetic code will differ, there is a unique genetic code for each species of living things. What are the odds against unintelligent chance bringing about the unique sequencing of the genetic code associated with each individual species of plant and animal life?[7] And in terms of our soulish and spiritual dimensions, what are the "chances" that chance could bring about phenomena such as the law of human nature or bring human personality from nonpersonality? It seems more in keeping with the second law to believe that these things were designed into us with the use of intelligence than that they "just happened."

Theoretical physicist John Polkinghorne, a colleague of

Stephen Hawking and president of Queen's College, Cambridge, is eminently known for his scholarship and brilliance in his field. He has been at the forefront of high-energy physics for thirty years. *Physics Bulletin* described his latest book, *The Quantum World*, as one of the best books of the genre.[8] Talking about scientific naturalism's view of origins, including its various speculations about the origin of the universe, Dr. Polkinghorne had this to say: "A possible explanation of equal intellectual respectability—and to my mind, greater elegance—would be that this one world is the way it is because it is the creation of the will of a Creator who purposes that it should be so."[9]

Like the first and second laws of thermodynamics, God's existence cannot be proven in any absolute sense. But like the first and second laws, his reality can be recognized through a process of logical reasoning from the wide variety of confirming observations from the natural world we live in and the laws of thermodynamics themselves. So, although like energy God might be invisible to the human eye, his existence can be detected by his many observable effects.

The Choice: Theism or Naturalism

The issue of origins is highly controversial. It is controversial, in part, because of its unparalleled importance to human existence, including our perspective when considering the nagging questions *Who am I? Why am I here?* and *Where am I going?*

There are two primary, competing theoretical models (or paradigms) related to the issue of origins: theism and naturalism.[10] In theism, God, the self-existent Being, is the Designer and Creator. In naturalism, nature is all there is; natural laws and chance, with sufficient time, are said to play the important role of designer. These two models, and their implications on our perspective of life, are very different.

Carl Sagan, a proponent of this second model, has

stated: "A Designer is a natural, appealing and altogether human explanation of the biological world. But, as Darwin and Wallace showed, there is another way, equally appealing, equally human, and far more compelling: natural selection, which makes the music of life more beautiful as the aeons pass."[11]

Is naturalism actually far more compelling than an intelligent Designer? When "natural selection" is described, words like *fate, accident, randomness,* and *chance* are almost always implied. Does that sound more compelling to you than the idea that an intelligent, benevolent God created the world and ourselves and that he has left traces of his actions everywhere?

Phillip Johnson, professor of law at the University of California at Berkeley and former clerk to the U.S. Supreme Court, suggests in his book *Reason in the Balance* that the most important statement in the Bible about creation is contained not in Genesis but in the opening verses of the Gospel of John.[12] These verses declare, "In the beginning was the Word, and the Word was with God, and the Word was God. He was in the beginning with God. All things came into being through him, and without him not one thing came into being."[13] The verses plainly state that Creation was by a force that was and is intelligent and personal. To espouse the opposite theoretical model, scientific naturalism, would require one to embrace unintelligent chance as the mechanism responsible for all things.

It's left up to the rational thinker, then, to decide which of the two competing origin models is the most compelling or indeed the most rational.

So, does God really exist? Look at the evidence—the almost incomprehensible amount of design all around us. It's there.

But there is yet more to be explored—something I call "experiential" evidence.

9

Heaven Intruding:
Personal Experience as Evidence for the Existence of God

> The experience of a miracle ... requires two conditions. First we must believe in a normal stability of nature, which means we must recognize that the data offered by our senses recur in regular patterns. Secondly, we must believe in some reality beyond Nature.
>
> —*C. S. Lewis (1898–1963)*

The question just does not go away: Is God real or a figment of our imagination? What we decide about this crucial question will have a significant influence on our worldview, including our ideas about the meaning and purpose of life. So, in an honest attempt to arrive at a rational position on the matter, it is important that we investigate the known sources of evidence on the subject.

We have already looked at several of these sources. What science has learned about our natural world provides a great deal of diverse and interesting evidence. The tenets and creeds of some of the world's religions present another type of evidence. But there are yet other sources of evidence in support of the reality of God. One of them is personal experience—experience that seems to have a supernatural touch going beyond the boundaries of chance, an intrusion from heaven for our well-being. Personal experience has a way of adding a special dimension to our understanding that we could not obtain in any other way.

There was a time in my life when I was unaware, or at least uncertain, whether an ordinary person could have an experience that might contain this supernatural touch. My worldview (my paradigms) had no place for it. As a result, I neither looked for nor sought such an encounter. Fortunately, however, when I was in graduate school, I met a person who shared with me some of his experiences. As I listened and saw the impact they had on my friend, I began to realize that perhaps there might be another way that God could demonstrate his reality—and do so at a very personal level.

You already know of my first recognized experience with God's intervention in my life. I told about it in chapter one. When I was hitting my head against a seemingly impenetrable wall in my doctoral research, God sent me a breakthrough in a sudden rush of insight. I was able to complete my research, receive my degree, and continue my academic career. But while that was the first time I was aware of God acting overtly in my life, it was far from the last.

In this chapter I am going to be sharing with you the stories of three other times in my life when I felt that God was intervening. These events were ordinary and yet not. As you read about them, you may declare to yourself, *Coincidence!* or *Mere intuition!* or even *Superstition!* If so, I must say these are understandable reactions for you to have—yet I don't in the least share them. Why? Because I was there. I wish I could convey to you the powerful sense I had, in each instance, of being touched by the supernatural. But I have no means to do so. Instead, first, I would urge you to ask yourself if there is a cumulative case to be made here by the recurrence of surprising events like these in a person's history (and these are by no means the only such I have had). And second, I would ask that, as you are reading my stories, you reflect on your own life, considering whether you, yourself, may have had similar experiences.

All this matters because, if God is truly acting in people's lives, then he—the one who invented and can circumvent entropy—must be real.

The "No Reason" Phone Call

One of the early obvious interventions by God in my life occurred at the outset of my academic career. It has had a profound effect on both my work as a professor and my personal and family life to the present day.

Shortly after successfully defending my Ph.D. thesis at the University of Illinois, Champaign-Urbana, I began looking for a job. I sent letters of inquiry and résumés to a number of engineering schools that I was especially interested in or that I knew were looking for new faculty. This resulted in a wide variety of invitations for on-campus interviews. Following the round of interviews, I began receiving some firm offers from a mix of respected schools. What an exciting time!

Now the real question was, how could I make the best decision from among so many good offers? From my earlier experience (the breakthrough in my doctoral research), I knew that God was interested in me at a personal level. Although I did not want to be presumptuous, I believed that if he were interested in my research, he would also be interested in helping me find the right job. June and I prayed that God would give us wisdom about which position I ought to accept.

Eventually, we narrowed the choice to two possibilities: the University of Maine and Oakland University. These two schools were very different. Although small, the University of Maine was more than a century old, having been established in 1865. In contrast, Oakland (located in Rochester, Michigan) was in its infancy. Not only were there no traditions at Oakland, but also there was no guarantee that the university's fledgling School of Engineering—only a few months old at the time—would even survive. The situation was all the more tenuous because Oakland's tiny engineering program would be competing against local giants: the University of Michigan, Michigan State, and Wayne State.

Furthermore, since June and I are lovers of nature and the out-of-doors, spending what time we can in canoeing, fishing, and hiking, the location of the University of Maine, in picturesque Orono, gave it an edge in our minds. The suburban Detroit location of Oakland University could not compete in this category. Of course, my natural bias for the University of Maine was further enhanced for me when, during my interview there, I was told that school holidays were declared on the opening days of both deer and trout season! But still, we did not jump into any decision.

One of the things that June and I have tried to do when making important decisions is to make them slowly. When we reach the point where we think we know the best decision, we sit on it for several days to see if it "feels" right. And so it was just prior to the new year when we finally came to the conclusion that I should accept the position at the University of Maine. This was on a Thursday. In keeping with our custom, we decided to wait until the following Monday before making it official. In the meantime, we asked God to confirm our decision or somehow show us if our decision was not the best.

We went on a short trip over the weekend as a means of stepping back from it all. It turned out to be one of those rare, beautiful winter weekends. A fresh snow had fallen on Friday evening, and Saturday dawned bright, sunny, and still. Every tree and bush glistened with snow-tipped branches. Hiking outside in the crisp, still air was a delight to all that made us human—spirit, soul, and body. We naturally assumed that the sense of peace we enjoyed, if it meant anything, was supposed to be a confirmation that we had made the right decision.

We arrived back in Champaign-Urbana late on Sunday evening, so it was not until the relatively late hour (for us) of 8:30 on Monday morning that we finally rolled out of bed. June and I briefly discussed our continued good feelings about the decision to go to Maine and asked God to block this outcome in some way if it was not right. At 9:30 I stepped into the kitchen to make the call to the chairman of the mechanical engineering department at the University of Maine. I stood in front of the phone for several minutes, gathering my thoughts so that my acceptance statement would sound both upbeat and intelligent. I even jotted a few choice words on a piece of paper.

Just as I reached for the phone, it rang. The unexpected sound startled me. When I recovered my presence of mind, I picked up the phone and answered. The voice on the other end said, "Hello, Gil. This is Jack Gibson from Oakland University." (Jack was dean of engineering.) After the normal exchange of greetings, he said with an apologetic tone, "Gil, I'm sorry to bother you. But as I was driving to the office this morning, I couldn't get you out of my mind. It wasn't anything specific, so I'm not sure why I'm calling. I thought that perhaps you might have a question or two about Oakland or about the job."

I thanked him for his sensitivity and consideration and assured him that I did not have any questions.

Again he apologized for not having had any clear reason for the call. Then he ended the conversation with these words: "Gil, please don't feel any pressure to decide. Take your time. I'm sure that what will be best for you will be best for Oakland."

I set the phone down with an unsteady hand. Then I said to June, who by then had walked into the kitchen, "We were just protected from making the wrong decision." Somehow, at the instant when Dean Gibson had identified himself, I had known with utter certainty that Oakland University's was the faculty position I should accept.

To this day, I cannot explain why June and I, prior to the unexpected phone call, had been so convinced that we should go to Maine. I suspect it was because of my natural bias—my paradigm, if you will—about the importance of its geographical location. The bottom line, however, is that (as I believe) God intervened on our behalf and helped us make what has turned out to be an extremely important career decision. I have never once second-guessed or regretted that decision made over thirty-five years ago.[1]

A Girl's Bike

Nine years passed since I began teaching at Oakland University, and we were living in Rochester Hills, our family now expanded by the addition of our two children: René and Ty. Early one snowy morning in late January, I was luxuriating in a hot bath at home. My comfort at this moment presented a wonderful contrast to the self-imposed suffering I had undergone up until a few minutes earlier, when I had come in from a three-mile run in the darkness with the wind buffeting my body and tiny pellets of snow seeking to drive themselves into my exposed face. Such morning runs have been a part of my life since my college days. (It breaks my heart to tell you this, but I'm not as fast as I used to be—the second law has seen to that.)

Lying in a warm tub after a hard workout has for many years been one of my most productive times for thinking. I don't know why. Perhaps it's because during the workout the brain benefits from the increased blood flow. Or maybe it's the quietness of the early morning before the rest of the family wakes. In any event, tub time is when I seem to do my most creative thinking. It's also a time when I both talk to and try to listen to God. I have never heard an audible voice, but I believe there have been times when I have thought God's thoughts. This particular day was one of those times.

Let me back up a little. My daughter, René, was approaching her ninth birthday. She had grown too big for her bicycle and needed a larger one. So I had gotten a used bike from a neighbor and was in the process of fixing it up for her. It was a Schwinn Sting Ray, a popular bike at the time, complete with three speeds and the model's most identifying feature—a "banana seat." I had taken the bike apart and replaced the worn-out ball bearings and tires and the shabby pedals and handlebar grips. I had then cleaned and polished the entire bike, part by part. The work was nearly finished. René had watched me working on the bike, so she knew that it was going to be a present for her birthday—a little over a week away.

My thoughts turned toward René's birthday as I lay there in the comfort of my bathtub after the run. I wondered if she was as excited about getting the new bike as I was about giving it to her. All of a sudden, interrupting those pleasant thoughts, there came an uninvited question into my mind: *Why don't you ask René if she really wants the bike?* It was a disturbing thought. I had worked hard on that bike during my spare time for over a month. It looked brand-new. How could any kid not want that bike? But I had learned not to discount such unexpected thoughts.

A short time later, I was dressed and standing in front of the bathroom mirror, getting ready to shave. Just then René walked past the open door, greeting me with her customary "Good morning, Dad." I quickly turned toward her and replied, "G'morning, Britches. Come on in." She bounded into the room with her ready smile and jumped up to sit on the long countertop that ran along the wall adjacent to the sink.

Looking into her twinkling blue eyes, I asked, "René, do you really want the bike I've been fixing up?"

She immediately glanced away, and there was a long

pause. I wondered what she was thinking, but I said nothing. Finally, she turned back and said in a soft, hesitant voice, "Dad, I don't know just how to say it, because I don't want to hurt your feelings—" There was another short pause, then she continued, "But I would rather have a girl's bike."

How stupid of me! Of course, the used Sting Ray was a boy's model. A nine-year-old girl would not want it.

René got a girl's bike for her birthday. In fact, we went down to the local Schwinn bicycle shop and she picked out the one she wanted that same week.

My view of this particular experience, as in the case of the phone call from Oakland's engineering dean, is again that it was a case of being protected from making a decision that was not the best. I know my daughter and her abhorrence of hurting anyone's feelings. If I had not asked her whether she wanted the old bike, she would probably never have told me her true feelings about it. I am grateful that Someone suggested I ask.[2]

Not long afterward, I would have a similar, yet even more unexplainable, experience in buying a present for my son.

Glove for a Left-Hander

In our younger days, June and I both played a lot of baseball and softball, so we had a pair of baseball gloves that we often used to play catch in our front yard. It was natural that we would teach our kids to throw and catch a rubber ball at an early age. They both got to be pretty good at it. There was just one problem with our arrangement. While June and I are both right-handers, our son, Ty, is a left-hander. So when he would try to put one of our baseball gloves on his little hand, the thumb of the glove would be on the inside rather than the outside.

One day when Ty was about seven years old, he asked, "Daddy, will you get me a baseball glove?" I looked at the size of his little hand and told him that it might be better to wait another year when he would be bigger. My explanation for waiting seemed to satisfy him, because whenever the subject came up, he would speak of it in terms of "next year, when I'm bigger." I didn't think much more about Ty's request until several nights later when I had a dream.

I dreamed that I was standing in a sports shop, looking at a large rack of baseball gloves that was hanging on a wall. There had to have been twenty-five or thirty different gloves on that rack. All of the gloves were the normal, rich brown leather—that is, all except one. The glove in the lower left-hand corner of the rack was made of black leather. When I looked more closely at the black leather glove, I recognized that of all the gloves on the rack, it was the only one made for a left-hander.

I woke up early the next morning, vividly remembering the dream. Not thinking anyone else was awake, I quietly got up and went into the kitchen. Suddenly, I heard the sound of little feet pattering down the hallway. It was Ty. He came bursting into the kitchen and said, "Daddy, I had a dream last night." With words spilling over like a waterfall, he told me that in his dream he had seen one of our right-hander gloves suddenly change into a left-hander glove. I immediately knew what all this meant and what I had to do.

I took off from work early that day so that I could be home when Ty got off the school bus. Without telling him why, I asked him if he would like to go with me to the store. He happily accepted my invitation.

We drove to town and began going to various sports shops. This may sound weird—bear with me here—but I walked into each shop looking for a rack of baseball gloves like the one I had seen in my dream. I was beginning to question my own sanity when finally I entered the fourth store and saw a rack of gloves that looked just like what I had seen in my dream, except that the rack was lying flat on a table rather than hanging on the wall. There was only one black leather glove on the rack. It was at the bottom left-hand corner.

It was for a left-hander.

Up until then, I had not told Ty what I was doing or what we were looking for. At that point, however, I pointed to the rack of gloves and asked him to pick one out. It did not take him long to locate the black leather left-hander's glove. I asked him if he would like me to buy it for him. When he mumbled something about waiting until next year when he was bigger, I told him about the dream I had had.

We bought that black leather baseball glove, even though Ty's little hand seemed to get lost inside it when he put it on. He slept with the glove for weeks. He used it during all his years of Little League and later when he played in a community softball league. In fact, Ty still has it today, twenty-four years later.

God the Willingly Found

You may be wondering why I chose to relate the last two experiences. I chose them because I think they demonstrate not only the personal character of God but also his interest in the smallest details of our lives. After all, in the total experience of Ty's life, how important was it that he got his own baseball glove at age seven rather than at age eight? I certainly did not think it was important. God, however, for reasons known only to him, must have thought it was important enough to take the initiative to get my attention. The same seems to be true about René and her bike. Furthermore, both of these experiences revealed to me something special about the heart of God that I will never forget—and neither will Ty nor René.

God let me find him in these experiences, and I will be forever grateful. He let me find him in an important career decision. He let me find him in a decision about what bike I should give my daughter. And he let me find him in a decision about when I should buy my young son his first baseball glove.

Experiences like the ones I have just related to you have been instrumental in the development of my convictions about the reality of God and his personal interest in me and my family. The experiential data I have accumulated over the years is not unlike the many examples found in the Bible in which people had definite contacts with God. Not as dramatic, for the most part, but nonetheless convincing. Of course, some of my experiences might be explainable simply in terms of the serendipity of natural circumstances. But all of them? I don't think so.

When I contemplate these confirming experiences, each has been unique in some way. There have been no duplications, and each experience has been at God's initiative. Sure, in some instances I had asked for his input, but I could not in any way have conjured them up, nor could I have demanded or earned them. They were simply a gift, given by a Father who wants us to find him.

When René and Ty were young, one of the games they liked to play with their daddy was hide-and-seek. I could have picked hiding places where they probably would never have found me. But I wanted my kids to find me. So I would choose my hiding places accordingly. Over time, my kids began to recognize my favorite hiding places, and they would always look there first.

In the Bible, God says, "If you search with all your heart, I will let you find me ..."[3] It seems that God really wants us to find him. Perhaps he expects us to learn to look for him in his favorite places—in the natural world that is all around us and in our personal experiences.

He also expects us to look for him in the special Book he has provided for us.

10

God's Self-Portrait: The Bible as a Source of Evidence about the Creator

> The Bible is a letter from God with our personal address on it.
>
> —*Søren Aabye Kierkegaard (1813–55)*

So far in this book, we have looked at some of the indirect evidence for God's existence. For example, we have considered the entropy-time curve of the universe with its initial point of minimum entropy (maximum order), the uniqueness of the second law (its negativity), the overwhelming amount of perceived design in the natural world (especially in living things), and the law of human nature (sense of right and wrong). We know, though, that no amount of empirically determined evidence can prove, in any absolute sense, the reality and existence of God. (The first and second laws are in the same category.) Still, taken as a whole, there is considerable indirect evidence for a God of the universe, and we cannot just push it all aside simply because we cannot see or touch him. Just as circumstantial evidence can support a reasoned conviction in a court of law, so circumstantial evidence can support a reasoned conviction about the existence of God.

If, however, we are trying to find God in the sense of learning about him, the indirect evidence is limited because it is impersonal. The indirect evidence provides us with insight into God's wisdom, intelligence, and power. But there is little information there about his personal characteristics.

(Although, if he was responsible for such creatures as the giraffe, armadillo, and duck-billed platypus, we know he probably has a sense of humor.)

I have shared some examples of personal experiences that I have had over the years. These experiences, without question, have enhanced my conviction not only that God is real but also that he is a personal God—a God who is interested in us as individuals. As valuable as personal experiences are, though, they are still limited in scope. If God really wants us to get to know him, in the same way we know a good friend, then we need more information about his personality and character than just glimpses. He needs to be more open with us, much as would the closest of our friends. So how else might God communicate to us what he is really like—close and up-front?

As we know, a major part of the communication difficulty we have is that God is a Spirit and thus normally invisible. A second difficulty is that the only other intelligent beings that we know (or we *think* we know) how to relate to are other humans. In this vein of thought, Francis Schaeffer—one of the most influential philosophers of the twentieth century—had this to say in his classic book *The God Who Is There:*

> In historic Christianity a personal God creates man in his own image, and in such a case there is nothing that would make it nonsense to consider that he would communicate to man in verbalized form. Why should he not communicate in verbalized form when he has made man a verbalizing being, in his thoughts as well as in communication with other men? Having created man in his own image, why should he fail to communicate to that verbalizing being in

such terms? The communication would then be three ways: God to man, and vice versa; man to man; and man to himself. Someone may raise queries as to whether in fact such communication has taken place, but in this field of reference, it is neither a contradictory nor a nonsense statement.[1]

If one accepts the assumption that God wants to communicate to humans in verbalized form, one still might ask *which* religious scripture contains his communication. There may be some truth in all the religious scriptures, but in my view, none of the others is in the same category with the Bible. There is a qualitative difference between this book and the others. You see this, for example, in relation to second law of thermodynamics. No other religious scripture that I know of describes entropy as aptly as does the Bible, saying, as it does, that "creation was subjected to frustration" and is in "bondage to decay."[2] More importantly, no other scripture gives a believable, self-consistent reason for the origin of this uniquely negative law, as does the Bible, saying it was imposed on nature by nature's Creator as a consequence of human rebellion—sin.[3]

I have found the Bible to be a book like no other, able to tell me things about God and myself that I could never learn from science or any other source. I hope to commend it to you. But before we get to the issues of why we should trust the Bible and what we can get out of it, I want to point out a surprising similarity between the study of thermodynamics in the scientific realm and the study of God in the theological realm.

Two Principles Times Two

In a typical thermodynamics textbook, the first portion deals with the first law; the second portion, with the second law. But there is still a rather thick portion of the book to be digested. What is the rest of the book about? The rest of the book is devoted to the implications and applications of these two major principles.

I find an interesting parallel here with the Bible. Like the typical thermodynamics textbook, the Bible contains two major principles: (1) There is a God of the universe, and (2) Jesus Christ is his Son.[4] Generally the first portion of the Bible, the Old Testament, is concerned with the first principle; the second portion of the Bible, the New Testament, is concerned with the second principle.

As with our textbook on thermodynamics, the Bible sets forth its two major principles rather succinctly, then leaves us with a good deal of material to be digested. What is the rest of the Bible about? Again as with the thermodynamics textbook, the balance of the Bible is devoted in some way to the implications and applications of its two major principles.

As it is with the first and second laws, if the two major principles of the Bible are principles of reality, then their implications and applications are of considerable importance to the human race. They are matters we are unwise to ignore. We need to search the Scriptures for what they have to tell us, so long as we are reasonably persuaded that these Scriptures are to be believed.

An Out-of-This-World Book

Considerable evidence exists that the Bible is much more than just an ancient book, that in fact it has a supernatural dimension. Among the categories of evidence, two are the Bible's uniqueness and its reliability.

One aspect of the Bible's *uniqueness* is its extraordinary combination of diversity of authorship and unity of perspective. The Bible was written over a fifteen-hundred-year time span and by more than forty different authors from every walk of life, including kings, peasants, philosophers, fishermen, poets, statesmen, and scholars. These forty authors wrote about hundreds of controversial subjects with amazing harmony and continuity.

How else can one explain the Bible's unity of perspective except by appealing to a divine superintendence of the writing? That is, although the authors of the Bible wrote out of their own situations, and reflecting their own personalities, God was invisibly at work, ensuring that everything they wrote was consistent with his truth. The Bible, in fact, makes this claim for itself.[5]

Another aspect of the Bible's uniqueness is seen in its circulation and translation. The Bible has been read by more people and published in more languages than any other book by far. The entire Bible (Old and New Testament) has been translated into 355 different languages, while the New Testament has been translated into another 880 different languages. Also, various portions of the Bible, such as the Psalms and Gospels, have been translated into still another 932 different languages. Therefore, the Bible or portions of it have been translated into a total of 2,167 different languages, which together represent the primary languages of more than 90 percent of the world's population.[6]

Global distribution of the entire Bible between the years of 1900 and 1998 is estimated to be 2.2 billion copies. Over the same period of time, 3.7 billion New Testaments were distributed. In addition, nearly 33 billion portions of the Bible have been distributed since the year 1900.[7]

As a comparison, the popular author Danielle Steel wrote forty-six best-selling novels between the years 1981 and 1998. According to her Web page, the total global distribution of the forty-six novels has been 370 million copies.[8] During the same time period, the global distribution of the entire Bible was an estimated 850 million copies (1.36 billion copies of the New Testament).

Year after year, the Bible has exceeded all best-selling books to such a great extent that it is no longer even mentioned as the best-seller. It is hard to explain this popularity in any other way than by presuming it has a supernatural influence on people.

Meanwhile, the Bible's *reliability* has been tested by comparing historical texts. For the Old Testament, this includes the famous Dead Sea Scrolls. Those scrolls—discovered in the 1940s in caves near Israel's Dead Sea—contain copies of Old Testament books dating as much as one thousand years earlier than any other copies we have. Yet the differences between the Dead Sea versions and the later copies are incredibly slight.

At the same time, we have many copies of New Testament books from the early Christian centuries. The earliest—a fragment of the Gospel of John—may have been written around a.d. 140. That's perhaps only half a century after the original of the Gospel was written. This fragment may, in fact, have been copied directly from the original.

We have much better evidence for the accuracy of our copies of the biblical documents than we have for any other ancient texts we use, including the poems of Homer, the astronomical research of Ptolemy, or the philosophy of Marcus Aurelius. We can trust that what we read in our Bibles is substantially the same as what was written by the original authors, with differences so minor as not to matter.

But beyond just the reliability of the texts themselves, we have extrabiblical confirmation for many historical events described in Scripture. For example, the first-century a.d. Jewish historian Flavius Josephus mentions the ministries of both John the Baptist and Jesus. The decree by the Persian emperor Cyrus to let the Jewish captives go free (mentioned in the book of Ezra) is preserved to this day on a writing cylinder. These are just a couple of the many examples of evidence that could be produced.[9]

Not all biblical claims have been, or can be, verified by other sources. Moreover, both biblical texts and archaeological findings are subject to interpretation. Yet the Bible demonstrably surpasses all other ancient religious scriptures in terms of being in harmony with other sources of facts.

As a scientist, I feel confident that I need not sacrifice the rigorous pursuit of truth just because I am a Christian. I can seek to understand what truly is, whether I seek it in nature or in the Bible, for the one God created both.

The Bible's Leading Man

I said earlier that the second of the Bible's two main principles is that Jesus Christ is the Son of God. In a sense, Jesus Christ is the culmination of everything the Bible is trying to say. As we look for evidences of the existence of God, we would be foolish to ignore the Son he sent as an earthly embodiment of his being.

The first four books of the New Testament, called the Gospels, focus on the life, teachings, and activities of Jesus. They also describe in considerable detail the personal relations and interactions that Jesus had with all types of people: peasants and kings, the poor and the rich. These four Gospels—Matthew, Mark, Luke, and John—give us four different viewpoints of Christ. The collective result is similar to that of a wise newspaper editor who sends out four different reporters to cover a significant event to ensure that nothing important gets missed.

Jesus himself indicated that one of the major reasons for his ministry was to reveal to humankind what God was like.[10] If this is true, then reading the Gospels will enhance our understanding of God—his personality and character.

Philip, one of Jesus' disciples, speaking not only for himself but also for others who were wrestling with the question of God's existence, asked Jesus one day to show them the Father.[11] (A question many of us would like to ask if given the opportunity.) At the time the question was asked, Philip had probably known Jesus for about three years. Jesus' response was a most astonishing claim: "Don't you know me, Philip, even after I have been among you such a long time? Anyone who has seen me has seen the Father."[12]

Speaking about Jesus, C. S. Lewis, in his own pungent fashion, expressed how really unique this claim was.

> On the one side clear, definite moral teaching. On the other, claims which, if not true, are those of a megalomaniac, compared with whom Hitler was the most sane and humble of men. There is no halfway house and there is no parallel in other religions. If you had gone to Buddha and asked him, "Are you the son of Bramah?" he would have said, "My son, you are still in the vale of illusion." If you had gone to Socrates and asked, "Are you Zeus?" he would have laughed at you. If you had gone to Mohammed and asked, "Are you Allah?" he would first have rent his clothes and then cut your head off.[13]

The historical evidence for the existence of Jesus Christ as a real person is overwhelming. No credible historian would dare try to pass him off as a mythological figure. So the controversy, which has raged for nearly two thousand years, is not focused on whether Jesus Christ existed but rather on whether he was who he said he was. This is a question each of us has to answer for ourselves.

Many non-Christians today who know about Jesus, including adherents of the other major world religions of Hinduism, Judaism, Buddhism, and Islam, recognize Christ as a great moral teacher. Some even consider him a great prophet of God. Taking into consideration everything that

Jesus taught and said about himself, C. S. Lewis comes to this challenging conclusion:

> Jesus … told people that their sins were forgiven. This makes sense only if He really was the God whose laws are broken and whose love is wounded in every sin. …
>
> I am trying here to prevent anyone saying the really foolish thing that people often say about Him: "I'm ready to accept Jesus as a great moral teacher, but I don't accept His claim to be God." That is the one thing we must not say. A man who was merely a man and said the sort of things Jesus said would not be a great moral teacher. He would either be a lunatic—on a level with the man who says he is a poached egg—or else he would be the Devil of Hell. You can shut Him up for a fool, you can spit at Him and kill Him as a demon; or you can fall at His feet and call Him Lord and God. But let us not come with any patronizing nonsense about His being a great human teacher. He has not left that open to us. He did not intend to.[14]

Let us not make the mistake of dismissing Jesus' claims with some kind of pious, but partial, approval. Far better to seek in Jesus the very nature of God. For then we can begin to know who we are and what God wants of us.

The revelation of God in the form of the Bible and in the form of his Son helps us trust that he loves us and wants the best for us, even though he had to impose negativity because of sin. Does it not seem reasonable that this sort of God would provide a way for us to escape the effects of entropy? That exciting prospect is what is in view in the next chapter.

11

Soaring Free:
How Spiritual Entropy Can Be Overcome
in a Person's Life

> Those who hope in the Lord
>   will renew their strength.
> They will soar on wings like eagles;
>   they will run and not grow weary,
>   they will walk and not be faint.
> —*Isaiah (eighth century B.C.)*

Early summer one year, my wife, June, and I took a trip west with our daughter, René, and son, Ty, to do some wilderness backpacking. Our destination was the Bridger Wilderness Area in the Wind River Range of the Rocky Mountains, in west-central Wyoming. René and Ty were in their early teens. We planned to spend a week hiking in the Green River Valley—first heading upstream along the river, and then climbing up and along the east side of Granite Mountain to a small lake located at an elevation of 10,300 feet. The scenic lake, surrounded on three sides by spruce and jack pine, was purported to be teeming with speckled trout.

As a school science project, just prior to our trip, Ty had researched and written a paper on the bald eagle—describing in detail its dramatic comeback as an endangered species, its varied habitat, its keen eyesight and its superb soaring ability. You can imagine Ty's delight when on the second day, as we were hiking along the river in a spectacular canyon of sheer rock, we suddenly spotted an eagle soaring in graceful circles directly above us. The eagle was silhouetted against a bright blue sky punctuated by white cumulus clouds. Watching through his binoculars, Ty could see that the bird's plumage was dark brown. He knew it was a bald eagle when it banked in the afternoon sunshine exposing its identifying white head, neck and tail feathers. The wingspan was easily six feet across.

If the bird was searching for prey, we could not detect it. In fact, the bird seemed to be simply enjoying the feeling of soaring effortlessly on the heated air that rose up the sides of the canyon walls. We marveled at the bird's ability to keep aloft with only small adjustments in its wings; it never once flapped. The bird seemed to be free of any constraint from the world below.

An eagle's apparent freedom from gravity offers as good an image as any of the freedom from spiritual entropy that we all, somewhere deep inside, long for. The time has come, in this chapter, to consider how spiritual entropy builds up in our lives and how we can zero it out.

Spiritual Things

First must come a clarifying of terms. I will be talking much in this chapter about spirit and spiritual things, and I don't want you to misunderstand because you don't know how I am using the key terms.

The words *spirit* and *spiritual* have a number of implied meanings. What we think about when we hear these words depends on their context as well as on our personal paradigms and experience. Sometimes, for example, the word *spirit* is simply used as a synonym for a person's demeanor. We might hear someone say, "She has a sweet spirit about her." What is normally meant by this phrase is that the person radiates a gentle, pleasant attitude. This is certainly a laudable attribute for any person to have; however, in the context of this chapter, the word *spirit* stands for much more.

By *spirit* and *spiritual* here, I am really referring to the nonmaterial part of reality. An example of this is the human spirit. The Bible describes humankind as having a spirit, a soul, and a body.[1] So the word *spiritual* encompasses ideas about the human spirit. Other examples include beings who, unlike ourselves, are all spirit. The Bible describes God as a Spirit and talks about angels and demons—spiritual beings with no permanent physical bodies. Therefore, God and his created spirit beings also fall under our broad category defined by the word *spiritual.*

If the God of the Bible is a reality, then "spiritual things" are as much a reality as "physical things." Certainly, they are more subtle, because they are not directly observable. But then, as we have seen, many of the physical things that have come to be readily accepted as reality by the scientific community are not directly observable either. If spiritual things are real, then there is a spiritual dimension to life that is just as real as the physical dimension, irrespective of our present paradigms on the subject. It is therefore reasonable to consider the spiritual implications of the entropy analogy.

We have been circling closer and closer to the meaning of spiritual entropy throughout the course of this book. Now let me give you a plain definition: *spiritual entropy is the result of the bent each of us has to create disorder in matters that pertain to God and spiritual things.* We have that bent because of the same event that caused the imposition of the second law's negativity in the first place: the sin of our earliest forebearers, Adam and Eve. The tendency has been passed down, generation after generation, and we are thus born spiritually entropic. Yet we cannot blame anyone besides ourselves. We each willingly express our tendency every time we choose to think or do or say something that is contrary to what God (who provides the standard of goodness) approves.

I mentioned Mother Teresa in an earlier chapter. Even the truly good people of the world like Mother Teresa are subject to spiritual entropy. In fact, it may be that the most spiritually pure people are also the ones who are most aware of their tendency to do wrong. We are all spiritually disordered and disordering. We all have a big problem to face, and it is inside us. If the Bible is true, compared with spiritual entropy, even the problem of physical entropy is of little account.

Wrongdoing, Wrongthinking

Spiritual entropy, in my way of thinking, is closely related to two other kinds of entropy, namely, ethical entropy and philosophical entropy. As we explore these aspects, we get a fuller understanding of what spiritual entropy is all about.

"Ethical entropy" describes the spiritual consequences that result from those things that we humans do, or do not do, that are counter to what we inherently know to be right to do. Our standard of measure might be the law of human nature, civil laws, or the Ten Commandments. If the Ten Commandments represent the original of C. S. Lewis's law of human nature (see chapter four), then morality would also come under a spiritual heading.[2]

The ethical facet of spiritual entropy is associated with such things as selfishness, greed, pride, deception, lawlessness, cheating, stealing, drug and alcohol abuse, pornography, unrestrained sex, violence, spouse and child abuse, murder, and terrorism. In a word, *sin*.

Personal experience, the news, history, and the Bible all point to the same truth: a tendency to sin is inherent in human behavior. The very existence of the Ten Commandments, civil laws, police, civil courts, and jails is corroborating evidence. Children do not have to be taught how to sin; it comes naturally to them. Ask any parent.

Furthermore, ethical entropy, like its physical counter-part, seems to have a cumulative nature. If this is true, our personal lives can become weighted down with an accumu-lation of ethical entropy and with accompanying feelings of guilt. Sometimes the burden of accumulated ethical entropy and guilt can become overwhelming. When it does, we often try a variety of means for getting rid of some of it—denying its existence, blaming others, blaming our environ-ment or society. This approach to divesting ourselves of our accumulated ethical entropy rarely, if ever, really works. To be sure, we may deceive ourselves for a time, but more often than not, the truth of the matter eventually catches up to us.

There is a more effective way of divesting ourselves of the guilt associated with at least some of the above activi-ties. If the sin was against some person, we can go to that person and ask for forgiveness, even making restitution if appropriate. Therefore, with the expenditure of human energy (and some pride), it is possible, at least for this kind of situation, to decrease our ethical entropy.

But what if the sin was against God? Is there a possibil-ity of forgiveness from that quarter? We will return to this important question shortly. For now, let's turn to the second facet of spiritual entropy.

Philosophical entropy is more subtle and potentially even more detrimental to the quality of our lives than is ethi-cal entropy. The reason for this is that philosophical entropy is related to confusion about, and blindness to, the reality of spiritual things, concepts, principles, and truths. Quite often, spiritual confusion and blindness are consequences of the accumulation of ethical entropy. One reason for this blind-ness to spiritual things is that our subconscious does not want to think about a holy God, because doing so only increases our awareness of the magnitude of our ethical entropy and accompanying guilt. This is a clear example of the "paradigm effect."

In a related way, the Bible gives a sobering description of how philosophical entropy can be compounded in our lives:

> The wrath of God is being revealed from heaven against all the godlessness and wickedness of men who suppress the truth by their wickedness, since what may be known about God is plain to them, because God has made it plain to them. For since the creation of the world God's invisible qualities—his eternal power and divine nature—have been clearly seen, being understood from what has been made, so that men are without excuse.
>
> For although they knew God, they neither glorified him as God nor gave thanks to him, but their thinking became futile and their foolish hearts were darkened. Although they claimed to be wise, they became fools and exchanged the glory of the immortal God for images made to look like mortal man and birds and animals and reptiles.[3]

We can see here a continually increasing confusion with respect to truth. Once truth is suppressed, thinking becomes futile and hearts become darkened. Then the person becomes self-deceived about wisdom, ultimately exchanging truth for a lie. The thought that this could happen is frightening. It could happen to me; it could happen to you.

Without considerable care and wisdom, one's philosophical entropy can increase. If not dealt with appropriately, a person's ethical entropy can continually accumulate as well. Because of this, and because of the fact that populations are increasing, the spiritual entropy of our world has a tendency to continually increase. This sounds strikingly similar to the observed behavior of physical entropy—thus the analogy to the second law.

The magnitude of spiritual entropy describes a spiritual state or condition, whether it is the condition of an individual, a family, a group, a nation, or the human race. Two sobering, personal questions surface here: "What is the magnitude of my own spiritual entropy?" and "What can I do about it?" Sooner or later, we have to take responsibility for our spiritual waywardness.

Such is the plight of the human race. It has been held in tight bondage to the physical dimension of the second law, and to the spiritual dimension of the entropy analogy, from the time of humankind's earliest rebellion until now. If God imposed the second law, God is the only one who can repeal it. Is there any hope?

Of Eagles and Hang Gliders

Just as there is no evidence that the second law has been repealed in the physical dimension, so there is no evidence that the spiritual dimension of the entropy analogy has been repealed. This is true even for those who believe Jesus Christ to be who he claims to be in the Bible. The apostle Paul, author of several of the books in the New Testament, said this in one of them:

> I find this law at work: when I want to do good, evil is right there with me. For in my inner being I delight in God's law; but I see another law at work in the members of my body, waging war against the law of my mind, and making me a prisoner of the law of sin at work within my members. What a wretched man I am! Who will rescue me

from this body of death? Thanks be to God—through Jesus Christ our Lord![4]

Notice the interplay Paul describes here, a kind of push and shove between two opposing spiritual forces. He is describing a tension between a negative force trying to pull him down (spiritual entropy) and a positive force trying to lift him up (his spiritual nature, which wants to obey the dictates of conscience). Then Paul ends with the question "Who will rescue me from this body of death?" The answer given is Jesus Christ. This scenario suggests that, although entropy has not been repealed, God has made a way for those who have allied themselves with Jesus Christ to escape from the deadly effects of the spiritual dimension of the entropy analogy.

What, exactly, is this way of escape? We begin to get the idea as Paul goes on to say, "Therefore, there is now no condemnation for those who are in Christ Jesus, because through Christ Jesus the *law of the Spirit of life* set me free from the *law of sin and death*."[5]

In this passage, two opposing spiritual laws are again mentioned. The "law of sin and death" seems to be a clear reference to the spiritual dimension of the entropy analogy. But what is this "law of the Spirit of life"? How is it that one spiritual law can set a person free from another spiritual law? To help us understand, let's consider an analogy of the interplay of two opposing physical laws: the law of gravity and the law of aerodynamics.[6]

Think about an eagle or a hang glider. Gravity acts as a downward (negative) force that pulls the eagle or hang glider toward the earth. Aerodynamics provides an upward (positive) lift force on the wings of the eagle or hang glider that opposes the force of gravity. This aerodynamic lift is developed as air flows both over and under a wing. The shape and orientation of a wing causes the average air speed flowing along the top surface of the wing to be greater than what it is along the bottom surface. The net result is a pressure difference that gives an upward aerodynamic lift. Therefore, in a sense, the law of aerodynamics sets the eagle and hang glider free from the law of gravity. Without aerodynamic lift, both the eagle and the glider would drop like a rock. So, the law of aerodynamics provides the eagle and the hang glider pilot a way of escaping from the law of gravity.

In an analogous manner, the law of the Spirit of life opposes the law of sin and death. The law of the Spirit of life is capable of setting believers in Jesus Christ free from the spiritually deteriorating influences of the law of sin and death, thus providing a way of escape.

In our analogy, neither gravity nor aerodynamic lift is visible. Yet no one doubts their reality, because we have all seen their effects. Likewise, neither the law of sin and death (the spiritual dimension of the entropy analogy) nor the law of the Spirit of life is visible. Yet we can know their reality because we can observe their effects.

If we say that the law of the Spirit of life is a type of spiritual counterpart to the law of aerodynamics, so what? Is this just an interesting metaphor, or is there some practical value to it? What are the benefits of coming to understand and learning how to use this law of the Spirit of life?

In the book of First John in the New Testament, we encounter this statement, which is both blunt in its accusation and bold in its offering: "If we claim to be without sin, we deceive ourselves and the truth is not in us. If we confess our sins, he is faithful and just and will forgive us our sins and purify [cleanse] us from all unrighteousness."[7] If we are conscientious at all, the first part of this statement hauls us up short. It challenges us to reevaluate our paradigms on the matter of sin. The verse implies that if we simply brush the challenge away like we would an irritating fruit fly, we run the risk of self-deception. No one in his or her right mind wants to be deceived, especially about truth. And to intentionally deceive oneself is even worse.

But what about this verse? Is it just a record of the antiquated musings of some ancient scribe, or is it a statement of truth? If the imposition of the attendant negativity of the second law, including its entropy analog, was God's response to humanity's rebellion, then God must take sin seriously. To "rebel" means to resist, to fight against, or to ignore authority. If God is real, and if the second law's negativity was imposed as a consequence of humanity's rebellion, then sin is a reality we must reckon with.

It is quite natural for us to want to ignore the concept of sin. Acknowledging its potential reality immediately places us in a position of having some obligations to a holy God— a God most human beings know very little about. However, as the above statement implies, simply ignoring sin because it makes us uncomfortable runs the risk of self-deception. If the Bible is any kind of authority, the consequences of self-deception on this matter overwhelm the discomfort of having some obligations to God.[8] This is especially clear when considering the offer made in the second half of the above quotation.

As a child, you (I hope) experienced forgiveness by your parents for sins you committed against them. And if you are a parent, I hope you have also had the experience of forgiving your children for sins they committed against you. However, as a parent, what would your response be toward your children if they simply chose to ignore any responsibility they had to you and if they disregarded the reality of any sins they committed against you?

The quoted reference from First John says clearly that if a person recognizes that he or she has sinned against a holy God, confesses his or her sins, and asks God for forgiveness, then God will forgive the person. This forgiveness, in effect, removes a person's accumulation of spiritual entropy.[9]

The Miracle of Forgiveness

We need to recognize what forgiveness is and what it is not. Forgiveness is not in any way condoning or excusing the sin. Forgiveness is person-to-person. You forgive the person, not the action. In fact, the person doing the forgiving, more often than not, must absorb the pain inflicted by the action. Forgiving means you will not seek retribution or revenge. True forgiveness will not hold a grudge. It is possible to forgive the sinner but still hate the sin. Also, forgiveness does not necessarily remove the consequences of the sinful action.

If a neighbor boy intentionally throws a rock through your picture window, your forgiving him does not repair the broken window. However, your forgiveness will undoubtedly be of considerable personal value to the young man. It will relieve his guilt and will pave the way for a continuing, or perhaps even a better, relationship between the two of you.

Forgiveness is not an easy thing to grant. It seems to go against our human nature. Of course, some things are easier to forgive than others. Many would say that forgiveness is a lovely idea—lovely, that is, until they have something to forgive. Perhaps that is why forgiveness is considered to be one of the most difficult Christian virtues.

Forgiveness, furthermore, is not something a person deserves but rather is an act of grace given by the person who was sinned against. In fact, forgiveness can *only* be granted by the person against whom the sin was committed. As an example, let's consider again the incident of the broken window. What would have been your response (or for that matter, the response of the guilty boy) if some stranger who just happened to be passing by your home at the time the rock was thrown said to the boy, "I forgive you for breaking that window"?

The same principle that forgiveness can only be granted

by the person against whom the sin was committed holds true when we are considering sin against God. The marvelous thing is that God (who, unlike us, never needs forgiveness himself) is willing to grant the forgiveness.

Remember my friend's father, Phil, whom I visited in the hospital when he was dying of cancer?[10] He was anguishing over the regrets of having lived his entire adult life ignoring the existence of the God of the Bible. In so doing, he was ignoring questions related to death, to life after death, and to heaven and hell. He was ignoring the question of whether he had any obligations to God that could only be carried out while he was alive. These questions, which seemed so unimportant to him during most of his life, now suddenly loomed as the only things of significance as he stared into the face of death.

Here is the rest of the story.

One of the things Phil wanted to talk about during the afternoon we met was whether the Bible held out any hope that God would forgive him for ignoring him all those years. We assured him that the Bible did just that, and in fact that it was overwhelmingly clear on the subject. The verses quoted above from First John were an example.

That afternoon, Phil asked God to forgive him of his sins, and in particular of the sin of ignoring him all those years. He did not try to defend or explain away his actions. He simply asked God to forgive him. I watched in amazement as Phil's tears of regret dramatically changed to tears of relief and gratitude. He had made peace with God.

Before he died, Phil personally experienced the supernatural removal of a lifetime accumulation of spiritual entropy. According to what his son told me later, this relief, gratitude, and the absence of fear continued right up to when Phil died, a few days later. The law of the Spirit of life had set Phil free from the law of sin and death. I cannot explain how it works. I simply witnessed its effects. It was an experience I will never forget.

If Phil's experience was not an example of overcoming the spiritually deteriorating influence of the entropy analogy, then I do not know what is. This does not mean that a person who has had an experience of asking for and receiving God's forgiveness will never accumulate any more spiritual entropy. Our spiritual entropy begins accumulating again whenever we violate God's standards, fail to see truth when we are exposed to it, or intentionally or unintentionally allow philosophical error (erroneous paradigms) to get mixed in with philosophical truth. Nevertheless, the availability of the forgiveness of sin is a demonstration of the law of the Spirit of life setting us free from the detrimental accumulating effects of the law of sin and death. No wonder that the Bible refers to it as the gospel (good news) of Jesus Christ.

Last-but-Not-Least Insights

Our comparison of the law of aerodynamics overcoming the law of gravity with the law of the Spirit of life overcoming the law of sin and death has proved useful in helping us to see how spiritual entropy may be overcome in a person's life. But before I finish, let me point out two additional insights that can be gained from the comparison. These insights have everything to do with the practical implementation of this chapter's learnings.

First, using the law of the Spirit of life to overcome the law of sin and death requires knowledge of its existence by the user, along with experience and skill in using it. Let's go back to our aerodynamical analogy to explain this.

The mere existence of the law of aerodynamics is no guarantee of its effectiveness or usefulness. Using it to effectively overcome the law of gravity requires knowledge of its existence by the user, along with experience and developed skill in using it. If you have ever watched an eagle soar as it gracefully cuts spirals among the rising air currents on a warm sunny day, or if you have ever observed an experienced hang glider pilot try to emulate an eagle, it is clear that both are keenly aware not only that the law of aerodynamics exists but also of how they can best use it.[11]

The principles of aerodynamics were hidden from humanity's understanding until the early twentieth century, but hope of their existence was encouraged every time people observed a bird to soar. This hope was the motivation for the persistent dream of one day being able to fly. Beginning with early experimental observations that led to the discovery of the law of aerodynamics, the dream has come true, ranging in scope from a hang glider to a state-of-the-art supersonic jet.

In the same way, the mere existence of the law of the Spirit of life is no guarantee of its effectiveness or usefulness. That means doing as Phil did: approaching God in humbleness to ask forgiveness. Only by the means God has provided—forgiveness through faith in his Son, Jesus Christ—can we escape our spiritual entropy. We have to actually *use* the law of the Spirit of life; otherwise, merely *knowing* about the law is an empty mental exercise.

Second, it is the Holy Spirit who supplies the energy that empowers the law of the Spirit of life. Again, our analogy helps us understand what this means.

The effectiveness of the law of aerodynamics to overcome the law of gravity is enhanced by the addition of energy. Eagles, for example, have an uncanny way of finding thermals and (as Ty and the rest of us observed in our opening story) have been known to soar for hours without ever flapping a wing.[12] When an eagle finds and moves into a thermal, the addition of energy in the form of the rising air currents, coupled with the law of aerodynamics, makes it accelerate upward against gravity.

A good hang glider pilot also knows about thermals.

The eagle, however, has an advantage over a hang glider pilot: if unable to locate a thermal, it can provide its own energy by flapping its wings. (That's why ultralights—hang gliders with motors—were designed.)

How does this energy metaphor relate to the ability of the law of the Spirit of life to overcome the law of sin and death? The word "Spirit" in this phrase appears to be a reference to God's Spirit, often referred to as the Holy Spirit. This implies that God, through the Holy Spirit, supplies the energy that empowers the effectiveness of the law of the Spirit of life.[13] We cannot eliminate our spiritual entropy on our own; we need energy from no less a source than God himself. With God's help, however, not only can our spiritual entropy be eliminated, it can be replaced by what the Bible calls the "fruit of the Spirit:" love, joy, peace, patience, kindness, goodness, faithfulness, gentleness and self-control.[14]

As fantastic as all of this is, however, if a person is a believer, that person has an active role to play in the behavior-changing process. And it *is* a process, not an event. God's forgiveness is an event, a one-time experience. A behavior-changing process, on the other hand, takes time. The reason for the required time is that detrimental habits and erroneous paradigms often need to be exposed and adjusted. Also, there is a need to gain knowledge of the law of the Spirit of life.

The amazing bottom line of all this is that God has provided a means for us to overcome the detrimental effects of the law of sin and death, just as the soaring eagle overcomes gravity. Even more amazingly, we have reason to hope for complete and permanent rescue from entropy—both physical and spiritual.

12

Reasons for Hope:
Why We Can Look Forward to Final
Deliverance from Entropy

> Our Lord has written the promise of the resurrection
> not in books alone, but in every leaf in springtime.
> —*Martin Luther (1483–1546)*

Picture a couple standing beside the open grave of their six-year-old child. The past few days have been a nightmare for them. It began when their daughter woke in the night, complaining of not feeling well. But she soon fell back asleep, so the parents thought little about it. In the morning, though, she lay cold in her bed. An autopsy would reveal a congenital heart condition. Now the parents are going through the unanticipated, unbearable process of seeing their once-lively, adorable little girl lying in a casket for her funeral and then being lowered into a grave and away from their sight for good.

Are the parents feeling peaceful because death is "natural"? After all, those who say, "Death is just a part of life," are—in a sense—right. Of course the parents are not feeling peaceful! They are grieving. They *hate* death, their daughter's death in particular. They feel a horror at this intrusive force that has snatched away one they cherished—and snatched away a part of their hearts in the process.

We might have a dispassionate view about death when it is happening to a stranger, but when it is happening to someone we love, we feel, deep inside, that it is *wrong, wrong, wrong!*

Where do we get that sense? You might think that, as creatures who have lived with entropy from the womb, we would feel comfortable with the inevitable outcome of entropy for human life: death. But instead we feel that, somehow, our lives should go on forever. (If we don't have that feeling, it's a sign of deadness or emptiness of soul.) Is that feeling wrong?

I believe that feeling is very much right. Moreover, I think it has been planted in our hearts by a God who made us for eternal life. Human beings would have lived forever if it had not been for that first sin and the consequent imposition of entropy by God. And despite our current bondage to entropy, a time is coming—get this now—when the second law will be repealed and people will never again have to experience the effects of entropy!

The End of Entropy

I make my bold claim about the end of entropy despite the fact that science can offer no hope that the second law of thermodynamics will ever be repealed. From all that science can see, the entropy of the universe will inevitably, inexorably tend toward a maximum until the universe is nothing but a cold, still, silent litter of dust. Sounds a lot like death, doesn't it? Recall the words of the famous astronomer Sir James Jeans: "There can be but one end to the universe—a 'heat-death.'"[1] And long before that heat death, human beings will be history. This conclusion causes some scientists to despair and others to hope without reason.

Given this state of affairs, it's worth exploring what the Bible has to say. Does it offer hope without reason, or does it offer reason for hope?

Look again at the key entropy passage in the eighth chapter of the book of Romans: "The creation was subjected to frustration not by its own choice, but by the will of the one who subjected it, in *hope* that the creation itself will be liberated from its bondage to decay and brought into the glorious freedom of the children of God."[2] Creation, personified here, is in a state of expectation. It is aware that the "children of God" (that is, followers of Jesus Christ) have been empowered to overcome the deteriorating effects of the spiritual dimension of the entropy analogy—the law of sin and death. In other words, the creation is "watching" those who know about and are effectively using the law of the Spirit of life to overcome the law of sin and death.

If in our own experience we have clearly seen an improvement in our spiritual and moral integrity as a result of the law of the Spirit of life setting us free from the law of sin and death, that experience becomes a tremendous source of hope. As a believer (and I say this with much gratitude to God), I am not the same person morally and spiritually that I was ten years ago. The moral and spiritual condition of my life is better—healthier, stronger, and with much less entropy. I believe that my wife, my children, and my close friends would confirm this. I still have a lot of room for improvement, but because of what I have already experienced, I have much reason for hope.

From my personal experience as both an engineer and a licensed pilot, I know that with some understanding and developed skill, the law of aerodynamics can be used to overcome the downward pull of the law of gravity. Likewise, from my personal experience as a believer, I know that with some understanding and developed skill, the law of the Spirit of life can be used to overcome the downward pull of the law of sin and death. The Bible anticipates the kind of hope these experiences generate: "Always be prepared to give an answer to everyone who asks you to give the reason for the hope that you have."[3] As believers, we find a great source of hope in our experience with God not only for the present but for the future as well.

And in terms of that hope, we are following in the

footsteps of the man I described in a previous chapter as "the leading man of the Bible."

The Promise of Easter

When Christians celebrate Easter, they are celebrating a clear-cut violation of the second law. Christ's resurrection represents a reversal of the second law—a decrease in entropy—and that's one reason why many people have difficulty in believing in the Resurrection. Consider, however, that the one who had the authority and power to impose the second law would be able to selectively suspend, reverse, or repeal it. To Christians, the fact of Christ's bodily resurrection is a great source of hope. Indeed, Christ's resurrection is the clearest indicator of all that there is hope for the eventual repeal of the second law and its negative consequences.[4]

The Bible also teaches that Jesus Christ will return to earth one day—a future event referred to as the "Second Coming." The New Testament contains a number of references to the hope of a general resurrection at the Second Coming of Christ.[5] One such is the following: "If the Spirit of him who raised Jesus from the dead is living in you, he who raised Christ from the dead will also give life to your mortal bodies through his Spirit who lives in you."[6]

Grain seeds were found in King Tut's tomb in Egypt, where they had lain dormant for three thousand years. When a few of those seeds were put into warm, moist soil, they germinated and sprang to life within forty-eight hours. Perhaps the activities of the Holy Spirit are like the mysterious power (life processes) that resides in a simple plant seed, causing it to spring to life when the conditions are right.

Along with its references to a general resurrection of the dead, the Bible also teaches that a day is coming when God will repeal the second law of thermodynamics with its attendant negativity. In the last book of the Bible, the book of Revelation, we find some clear references to a future time when people will live in an environment without the *curse* of the second law hanging over their heads.[7] The apostle John was given the following glimpse into that future and place:

> I saw a new heaven and a new earth, for the first heaven and the first earth had passed away. ... And I heard a loud voice from the throne saying, "Now the dwelling of God is with men, and he will live with them. They will be his people, and God himself will be with them and be their God. He will wipe every tear from their eyes. There will be no more death or mourning or crying or pain, for the old order of things has passed away."
>
> He who was seated on the throne said, *"I am making everything new!"* Then he said, "Write this down, for these words are trustworthy and true."[8]

We can't know what life without entropy will be like, any more than we can be sure what an entropy-free life was like for the first humans before the Curse. Passages like the one from Revelation give us tantalizing glimpses of that existence. Also, Jesus' activities on earth after his resurrection—entering a locked room, rising up in the air—suggest freedom from normal constraints.[9] Thus, as a minimum, we know that our resurrection existence will be filled with life and activity, but without the sort of degradation that energy use now entails. Probably the best we can do is picture in our minds the greatest possible kind of life we can imagine—and then assume that life in heaven is much, much greater.

Maximum Spiritual Entropy

And now I have to say something that I would rather not.

Not everyone will get to experience the kind of joyful, entropy-free life that I have described. Some will, in fact, experience its opposite: maximum spiritual entropy. Eternal death, not eternal life.

I would like to believe that all people go to heaven, or at least that most of us do and that the rest, the really wicked, are annihilated body and soul—poofed out of existence. I don't want to believe in a suffering that can never end. But if I believe the Bible about the entropy law, about God and his Son, and about heaven, I have to believe the Bible when it describes hell.

If you find the idea of hell hard to swallow, then I can assure you that I sympathize. But I must ask you to consider whether it makes sense. The parents of the dead six-year-old child surely found their loss hard to swallow—*but it was true*.[10] Many things we don't want to believe are true. Evil and its punishment are as real as the second law of thermodynamics.

In case it may help, let me share with you how C. S. Lewis described hell, since it has helped me. Lewis said that some people choose to do without God—and in death as in life, they get their wish.[11] Hell is separation from God.

The difference between those who get to experience zero spiritual entropy versus those who face maximum spiritual entropy is whether the law of the Spirit of life is operative in their lives. For those who continue to live under the law of sin and death, never soaring free from spiritual entropy, their course trends in one direction—downward—until after death they arrive at their own spiritual "heat death."[12]

I said in the introduction that this book would be dealing with some serious issues. This warning is the most serious of them all.

A Hope That Lasts

The good news, the thought that cleanses our minds

from the horrors of hell, is that deliverance from spiritual entropy can be ours for the asking. As we have seen, spiritual entropy is a consequence of the natural bent toward wickedness that all of us are born with. For those who give up the futile task of trying to reduce spiritual entropy in their lives on their own and instead go to the One who imposed the entropy analog (or more specifically, go to the representative he sent to earth to provide *the way*: his Son, Jesus) for help with the problem, the spiritual entropy begins to lift. From God's perspective, the spiritual entropy is in fact already gone. As a practical matter, though, the removing of philosophical entropy (wrong thinking and bad habits) requires a renewing of our minds.[13] This is a lifelong cooperative process between God and the person.[14] That process of release from all forms of spiritual entropy is instantly completed upon physical death. The dead body is surrendered to physical entropy, but the living soul is free from spiritual entropy entirely. And one day, at the return of Jesus Christ to earth to culminate history, believers' souls will be reunited with their resurrected bodies, so that they are whole again and free from entropy both physically and spiritually—forever.

How beautifully the Bible's explanation of the imposition of entropy at the start of human history and its promise of the destruction of entropy at the end of history fit together! It's what scientists describe as an "elegant" solution, meaning it is simple and satisfying. What science cannot tell us about entropy, the Bible supplies.

This, then, is the hope the Bible gives us: an eventual rescue from physical and spiritual entropy (not to mention social, relational, moral, philosophical, emotional, and psychological entropy). And let's not undervalue the benefits of hope. Hope is a necessary ingredient for a healthy, productive life. Hope is a source of stamina to endure hard times. Hope sustains us till the end.

Yet what we are offered is more than just hope. If God imposed the second law, and if the Bible expresses the mind of God, then the hope expressed here is much more than a source for psychological well-being. It is *reason* for hope. The couple who lost their six-year-old child may never be entirely free of their grief in this life. However, they are Christian believers (as was their daughter), and so they have genuine reason to hope that their daughter is alive and well in a better world, where they will one day rejoin her.

If you do not have hope for freedom from death, the ultimate in entropy, but you see the reason for hope offered in the Bible, I invite you to invoke the law of the Spirit of life for yourself. As you do, you will begin to see your life changing, the level of spiritual entropy in your life dropping, just as has occurred for me and countless others. These encouraging indicators will greatly enhance the quality of your hope and assure you that your hope is not in vain.

Physical entropy is a burden we all bear in this life, but it need not be one we live with in the life to come. And spiritual entropy is a burden we need not bear even in this life.[15]

Conclusion

❧·❧

The second law of thermodynamics is the fundamental principle behind why ice cream melts and people age, why soup cools and cars rust, and in general why the quality of things seems to go downhill. Because of the law's pervasiveness, it is important for us to understand what we can and cannot do about it. First of all, we cannot avoid it, and it would be unwise for us to try to ignore it, since we will encounter both the second law and the entropy analogy many times every day of our lives. We can, however, benefit by learning from and exploring their many and diverse implications.

Although we cannot escape the second law or the entropy analogy, there are some things we can do to minimize their detrimental effects. For example, we can do a self-evaluation as to whether our involvement in relationships tends to bring order or disorder to those relationships. In other words, how do we, as individuals, affect the amount of entropy increase within our personal spheres of influence?

Furthermore, we can think about our individual lifestyles. Are we living in the fast lane and burning the candle at both ends? What about the nutritional quality of our eating habits, or for that matter, the nutritional quality of our "soul food," which nourishes the social, moral, and spiritual dimensions of life? There *are* things we can do about these things. God has also provided a well-designed plan for overcoming the spiritual dimension of the entropy analogy. We may opt in or we may opt out. It's our freedom of choice, our decision, our behavior, our life.

Perhaps you have been exposed to new ideas in this book. If so, let me appeal to you to not just walk away from them. Think about them. In fact, I hope that you will think about some aspect of the second law or the entropy analogy every time you have a personal encounter with either of them. You need to be careful, though, that you are honest with yourself in your thinking—that your reasoning is logical and sound. Be open to revising your paradigms, and do it the best way you know how.

If you have little or no familiarity with the Bible, you would benefit from obtaining a modern English translation and reading it, starting in the New Testament—say, in the Gospel of Mark—and then perhaps going to the book of Proverbs in the Old Testament before returning to the New Testament.[1] I have personally found the Bible to be a trustworthy source and standard for adjusting my paradigms about life. As we read the Bible, it is helpful to ask God to reveal his reality to us. If he is the inspirational author of the Bible, then he can be found there, just as he can be found in the life of Christ, in the overwhelming evidence of design in the natural world, and in personal experiences.

Maybe you are familiar with the biblical terminology I have used in this book but are short on personal experience with God. For example, you might not be convinced that you have personally experienced God's reality or that you have personally experienced a decrease in the spiritual entropy of your life. If this is your situation, I encourage you to evaluate your level of biblical understanding and your commitment to your faith.

Regardless of where you are in your spiritual journey, find someone you can talk to about it, preferably a Christian who is further along in the journey than you are. You and I are not just physical beings. There is a spiritual dimension to our lives that is just as real as the physical. Don't ignore it.

The most important and influential thing anyone can do, if not a believer, is to seriously consider the claims of Jesus Christ. Is he who he claimed to be? Depending on what we finally decide about this issue, we can have our spiritual entropy removed—not just once but any time it begins to build up. As we better understand the law of the Spirit of life, we will begin to see firsthand, in many different and exciting ways, how it sets us free from the spiritual dimension of the entropy analogy—the law of sin and death.

Just as the study of aerodynamics augments a pilot's abilities, so we need to study and learn about the law of the Spirit of life. In the process, we will find that the quality, meaning, and purpose of our lives can be greatly enhanced in every realm—physical, psychological, emotional, social, ethical, relational, philosophical, and spiritual. The resulting personal experiences will be a tremendous source not only of hope for our present lives but also of hope for that future day when God will repeal the second law, with all of its attendant negativity, including the entropy analogy.

That is what I have found, and what I continue to find, to be true.

An Unlikely "Coincidence"

In chapter one, I told how, as a grad student, I read a textbook that commented in passing on the philosophical implications of the second law of thermodynamics. I told also how this brief comment inspired my career-long search to understand those implications. That textbook I read back in 1965 was written by Gordon Van Wylen.[2]

About the time I was completing the first draft of the manuscript for this book, it occurred to me that it would be helpful if Dr. Van Wylen were to read and comment on it. But would he be willing? Was he even still alive?

I knew that, at the time I had been studying his book, Dr. Van Wylen was dean of engineering at the University of Michigan in Ann Arbor. And I knew that, seven years later, in 1972, he went to Hope College in Holland, Michigan, to become the college's president. But I had heard that he had retired back in 1987, and so I did not know where he might currently be living. My desire to have him read my manuscript thus seemed to be going nowhere. But for those of us who are attempting to follow him, God has a habit of working things out in ways we could never have imagined.

It was right about that time that my wife and I went to a three-day Christian conference in Indianapolis, Indiana. It was a big conference. The main auditorium held some forty-five hundred people.

On a fifteen-minute break, during one of the afternoon sessions, I struck up a conversation with the man seated on my right. His name was Bob. We chatted briefly about the conference, the great speakers, and the value of what we were hearing. Then we began to inquire a little into each other's personal lives—our families, our jobs, and so on. It was a normal conversation that soon became extraordinary.

When I told Bob that I was a professor of engineering and taught courses in the fluid and thermal sciences, Bob asked if I taught thermodynamics. I said that I did. He then asked me if I was familiar with a textbook written by Gordon Van Wylen. I told Bob that I was. Then I inquired, "Why do you ask?" His response was simple: "Because I have breakfast with Gordon almost every Saturday."

What are the odds that, just when I wanted to get in touch with Gordon Van Wylen but did not know how, I would sit next to one of his close friends in a crowd of four thousand-plus? Sometimes there is an "intelligent design" to the events of our lives.

Within a few weeks, Bob had put me in contact with Dr. Van Wylen, who, to my delight, agreed to read my manuscript whenever it was ready. Several months later, I sent him a copy. I had been right. Dr. Van Wylen's comments and suggestions were not only helpful; they were very encouraging as well.

Even more encouraging to me was this additional confirming evidence that God is interested and involved in my life. He was interested in my life when I was a doctoral student struggling to find a theoretical model that explained my experimental data. He has shown his interest in surprising ways at key points in my life all along, and he continues to show his interest. The journey I have been on with him has been an exciting adventure. It has not only filled me with hope, but given me reason for hope for what lies ahead in this life and beyond.

The Never-Ending Adventure

I invited you in the introduction to this book to come along with me on a journey of discovery about entropy in general, and spiritual entropy in particular. And if you have reached this point, you have indeed faithfully traveled with me. I hope your eyes have been opened to what Jeremy Rifkin called the supreme law of nature. And I hope you have seen that the entropy analogy reveals much that is profound about God and our souls. As Bible commentator G. Campbell Morgan has stated, nature is a great parable.[3] Certainly the negativity aspect of entropy tells us much about the sin problem that is all-important for humankind to consider.

But what is even more important is that you continue the journey, not with me, but with God. If you are willing, He is prepared to keep revising your paradigms about life so that they conform ever more closely to the truth. He is eager to take you, in fact to accompany you, from wherever you are on your spiritual journey toward a destination greater than you can imagine. You can be rescued from spiritual entropy and live with an amazing peace and in the glory and delight of spiritual freedom—forever.

Notes

❧·❦

Introduction

1. Although, strictly speaking, there is a clear difference between "the entropy law" (the apparent cause) and "entropy" (the effect). For simplicity of expression, the single word entropy will often be used for both—context will be the distinguisher.

2. You have a right to know where I'm coming from on these matters. I'm a Christian of the sort known as "evangelical," meaning I consider the Bible to be true and believe that Jesus Christ is who he claimed to be in the Bible. Having said that, however, I want to assure you that I respect everyone's right to believe as he or she wishes. I also understand that everyone is on his or her own spiritual journey and needs time to work through the issues. I have faith that, if someone is truly seeking the God who is, and not the god they want, that person will in time find him. I, myself, have arrived at my beliefs through a lengthy journey, and thus I feel comfortable in encouraging people to seek

the truth about Christ in their own journeys. "Seek and find" is advice common to both science and the Bible.

3. Joel Arthur Barker, *Discovering the Future: The Business of Paradigms* (St. Paul: ILI Press, 1989), 42. Although the quote was taken from the above reference, the concept was originally stated in a different context in Thomas S. Kuhn, *The Structure of Scientific Revolution,* 2d ed. (Chicago: University of Chicago Press, 1970), 150.

4. Barker, 59–60.

Chapter One: Mind Flood

1. As of this writing, I have been awarded a three-year research grant from the National Science Foundation to study a new application—two-phase condensing flow instabilities in multitube condensers. The fundamental theoretical model for studying this new application is—you guessed it—the original System Mean Void Fraction Model.

Chapter Two: Why Ice Cream Melts

1. The choice of this word was important to Clausius. It came from the Greek word, τροπη, meaning "transformation." In 1865 he wrote, "I have intentionally formed the word *entropy* so as to be as similar as possible to the word *energy;* for the two magnitudes [physical quantities] to be denoted by these words are so nearly allied in their physical meanings, that a certain similarity and designation appears to be desirable." Rudolf Clausius,

The Mechanical Theory of Heat (London: John VanVoorst, 1867), 357.

2. The word "universe" here is meant to include all of the physical universe that is or can be known. Therefore, from the perspective of science, it would be considered an isolated system.

3. Clausius, 365–6.

4. In this context, the word "surroundings" refers not just to other rooms but to everything outside of the specific room (system) under consideration.

5. Stanley Angrist and Loren Hepler, "Demons, Poetry, and Life: A Thermodynamic View," *Texas Quarterly,* September 1967, 30.

6. Quoted in G. Tyler Miller Jr., *Energetics, Kinetics, and Life: An Ecological Approach* (Belmont, Calif.: Wadsworth, 1971), 46.

7. Although I personally do not agree with all of Rifkin's philosophy, he has a clear understanding of the second law.

8. Jeremy Rifkin with Ted Howard, *Entropy: A New World View* (New York, Viking, 1980), cover jacket.

Chapter Three: Our Dark Shadow

1. My brother told me this true story of his experience when, during my younger days, we both worked for the same heating and air conditioning company.

2. As a law of nature, the second law represents science's description of a physically observed and repeatable pattern of behavior. Like other natural laws, the pattern is so consistent that the law has the *appearance* of a governing power, rather than simply being *evidence* of a governing power. Philosophically, there is a significant difference in the two perspectives. It is, however, this *appearance* of a governing power for which scientists use words such as the *influence, effect,* or *consequence* of a natural law; for example, the influence, effect or consequence of gravity. When such terminology is used in this book, it will be used in this manner.

3. Quoted in Jeremy Rifkin with Ted Howard, *Entropy: A New World View* (New York: Viking, 1980), 48. It appears to have been stated by Sir Arthur Eddington himself in *The Nature of the Physical World*, 1928.

4. I cannot take this thought very far since psychology is not my field. But it seems to me that a psychologist could do fruitful research in this area of "psychological entropy."

5. The words "intelligently processing," as used here, do not mean that the living thing is intellectually involved in the process, but rather that the life processes involved are so astoundingly complex and interrelated that they have the appearance of an intrinsic intelligence.

Chapter Four: The Entropy Analogy

1. Nancy Sullivan Geng, "Teardrops of Hope," *Reader's Digest*, September 1997, 76–77.

2. In this light, it is interesting that the expenditure of human effort to decrease the *social* entropy within some domain will necessarily cause an increase in the *physical* entropy outside that domain. This observation would appear to support the notion that analogical entropy might really *be* entropy

3. See Judg. 17:6; 21:25, New International Version.

4. C. S. Lewis, *Mere Christianity* (New York: Macmillan, 1969), 19. Lewis was professor of medieval and Renaissance literature at Cambridge University and had a prolific writing career. He wrote scholarly works of literary criticism, fantasy and novels, and theological and apologetic treatises in defense of historic, orthodox Christianity. More than 40 million copies of his books are in print.

5. Scott R. Burson and Jerry L. Walls, *C. S. Lewis and Francis Schaeffer: Lessons for a New Century from the Most Influential Apologists of Our Time* (Downers Grove, Ill.: InterVarsity Press, 1998), 23–34.

6. Lewis, 33.

7. Ibid., 21–26.

Chapter Five: Time Curve

1. There is also a transformation from chemical energy in our food to an electrical energy and to a chemical energy associated with our nervous system, as well as to another type of chemical energy associated with muscle contractions.

2. James Jeans, *The Mysterious Universe* (New York: Macmillan, 1944), 15.

3. Jeremy Rifkin with Ted Howard, *Entropy: A New World View* (New York, Viking, 1980), 49.

4. One curious implication of this hypothesis is that it suggests time may run forward and backward and forward again in an unending cycle, like a videotape on Play and then Rewind. In that case, you may have already read this note an infinite number of times.

5. In a book entitled *Is the World Running Down?* Gary North provides an interesting historical summary of this philosophical issue in a chapter dealing with "The Pessimism of Scientists." Gary North, *Is the World Running Down? Crisis in the Christian Worldview* (Tyler, Tex.: Institute for Christian Economics, 1988), 40–66.

6. To me, this uniqueness of the second law is its most intriguing characteristic. It was one of the reasons I was initially drawn to study the extended implications of entropy.

Chapter Six: Truth Matters

1. "Edward Smith" is the pseudonym I have given this real individual.

2. The dictionary defines *principle* as "truth that is a foundation for other truth." This certainly fits the first and second laws. This definition, however, is not limited to scientific principles.

3. It should be recognized, however, that if the God of the Bible is really God, then he can directly reveal himself or manifest his reality to anyone at any time and in any way he chooses.

4. The word "experiential" is used rather than "experimental" to indicate that the observation and verification process, although similar, is not necessarily the same as what it would be in the domain of science.

5. Jer. 29:13-14, New English Bible.

6. Remember that the second law was not recognized as a fundamental law until 1865, but that humans had been experiencing its influences all along.

7. The names "John" and "Phil" here are pseudonyms for real people.

Chapter Seven: The Curse

1. Recall that secondary models are based on one or more fundamental laws. Therefore, for a secondary law or model, science *does* have a means for addressing questions like why it exists or why it behaves in a particular manner. Its existence and behavior are traceable back to the fundamental law or laws upon which it is based. But science cannot trace fundamental laws back to anything else. From science's perspective, they "just are."

2. Gen. 1:4, 10, 12, 18, 21, 25, NIV.

3. Gen. 1:31, NIV, emphasis added.

4. I realize that many consider the story of Adam and Eve to be a mere myth, a fiction invented by humans to help explain certain conditions of human life. And if you are inclined to look at the story that way, I certainly respect your right to do so. However, I would like to point out that science is making it more "respectable" than ever to accept the reality of Adam and Eve, for genetic research suggests that human beings in fact are all the progeny of a single pair of ancestors. This chapter treats Adam and Eve as real people who were involved in real events that had actual effects on the human condition.

5. Gen. 3:17-19, NIV.

6. Rom. 8:20-21, NIV.

7. The book of Romans was written around the middle of the first century (about a.d. 57). This would place it eighteen centuries before Clausius coined the word *entropy.*

8. I'm not the only one to recognize this possibility. For example, J. M. Boice, F. F. Bruce, D. Martyn Lloyd-Jones, Henry Morris, John Murray, and John Stott have also recognized this possibility. Boice, Lloyd-Jones, and Morris mention the second law by name; the others imply it by description. J. M. Boice, *Romans* (Grand Rapids, Mich.: Baker, 1992), 2:872–4; F. F. Bruce, *The Epistle of Paul to the Romans: An Introduction and Commentary* (Wheaton, Ill.: Tyndale, 1963), 168–9; D. Martyn Lloyd-Jones, *Romans: An Exposition of Chapter 8:17-39: The Final Perseverance of the Saints* (Grand Rapids, Mich.: Zondervan, 1976), 55–57; Henry Morris, *Creation and the Modern Christian* (El Cajon,

Calif.: Creation Life Publishers, 1985), 148–50; John Murray, *The Epistle to the Romans: The English Text with Introduction, Exposition, and Notes* (Grand Rapids, Mich.: Eerdmans, 1960), 303–5; and John Stott, *Romans: God's Good News for the World* (Downers Grove, Ill.: InterVarsity Press, 1994), 238–41.

9. In this light, the magnitude of the negative influences of the second law, as we experience it, is probably more significant than we realize.

10. We considered social, relational, and ethical entropy in chapter four. We are now in the process of building a picture of spiritual entropy, which will be completed in the book's final two chapters.

11. Conceivably, if the second law did not exist at all between the start of Creation and the imposition of the curse, unidirectional physical mechanisms like heat transfer, mass diffusion, and chemical reaction could have been governed by a different law, perhaps one that God put in place provisionally before imposing the second law. But this is pure speculation without any evidence to support it.

12. Lost or blurred biological information could also make us (and living things in general) more susceptible to disease.

13. Matt Ridley, *Genome: The Autobiography of a Species in Twenty-Three Chapters* (New York: HarperCollins, 2000), 196–8.

14. This suggestion is speculation only. Yet biblical support for the idea is perhaps symbolized by the "tree

of life" referred to in the first and last books of the Bible (Gen. 3:22; Rev. 22:1-3, NIV).

Chapter Eight: Designer World

1. See chapter five, pages 60-64.

2. Parker H. Badger, *Equilibrium Thermodynamics* (Boston: Allyn & Bacon, 1967), 87–106.

3. Rudolf Clausius, *The Mechanical Theory of Heat* (London: John VanVoorst, 1867), 365–6.

4. Ravi Zacharias, *A Shattered Visage: The Real Face of Atheism* (Grand Rapids, Mich.: Baker, 1990), 12–13.

5. A few of the individuals associated with the ID movement include Michael Behe, William Dembski, and Michael Denton. The following books offer excellent introductions into the intelligent design approach: William A. Dembski, *Intelligent Design: The Bridge between Science and Theology* (Downers Grove, Ill.: InterVarsity Press, 1999); Michael J. Denton, *Nature's Destiny: How the Laws of Biology Reveal Purpose in the Universe* (New York: Free Press, 1998); Michael A. Behe, *Darwin's Black Box: The Biochemical Challenge to Evolution* (New York: Free Press, 1996).

6. The phrase "irreducible complexity" was coined by Michael J. Behe. Behe presents a powerful argument that irreducibly complex machines and systems are best interpreted as a result of deliberate intelligent design. Michael J. Behe, "Intelligent Design Theory as a Tool for Analyzing Biochemical Systems," in *Mere Creation:*

Science, Faith, and Intelligent Design, ed. William A. Dembski (Downers Grove, Ill.: InterVarsity Press, 1998), 177–81.

7. This apparent contradiction to reason becomes even more evident when we consider the total number of different, known species of plants, insects, fish, birds, and mammals, each with their own unique DNA code (genome). There are, for example, between four and five thousand known species of mammals, eighty-six hundred living species of birds, well over one million known species of insects, and thousands of species of fish (over five thousand species of the bony class alone). Maurice Burton, *Systematic Dictionary of Mammals of the World* (New York: Crowell, 1962), 5; *Encyclopaedia Brittanica,* 15th ed., s.v. "bird," "insect," "fish."

8. Cited in Zacharias, 42.

9. John Polkinghorne, *One World: The Interaction of Science and Theology* (London: SPCK, 1986), 79–80.

10. The primary model in the Western world is scientific naturalism. But worldwide, the theism model is the common ground of all creationists—Christian, Jewish, and Islamic. Adherents of these three religions are estimated to represent over 58 percent of the world population. The statistical global population data for 1998 (expressed in billions and rounded to two decimal places) is as follows: Christians, 1.97; Muslims, 1.18; nonreligious, 0.77; Hindus, 0.77; Buddhists, 0.36; atheists, 0.15; other religions, 0.18; Jews, 0.02. This data was obtained from David B. Barrett and Todd M. Johnson, "Annual Statistical Table on Global Mission: 1998," *International Bulletin of Missionary Research*

22, no. 1 (1998): 26–27. The magnitude of many of the above numbers is confirmed by John Bowker, *World Religions* (New York: DK, 1997), 190.

11. Carl Sagan, *Cosmos* (New York: Ballantine, 1985), 18.

12. Phillip E. Johnson, *Reason in the Balance: The Case against Naturalism in Science, Law, and Education* (Downers Grove, Ill.: InterVarsity Press, 1995), 107–8.

13. John 1:1-3.

Chapter Nine: Heaven Intruding

1. During those same thirty-five years, both Oakland University and its School of Engineering and Computer Science have grown by nearly a factor of ten. Also, an increasing number of Oakland's faculty are internationally recognized for their research.

2. None of my hard work on that Sting Ray was wasted. René's younger brother, Ty, was ecstatic when he was given the bike on his birthday, just one month later.

3. Jer. 29:13, New English Bible.

Chapter Ten: God's Self-Portrait

1. Francis A. Schaeffer, *The God Who Is There* (Downers Grove, Ill.: InterVarsity Press, 1998), 118.

2. Rom. 8:20-21, New International Version.

3. Gen. 3.

4. Although these principles are not fundamental scientific principles like the first and second laws of thermodynamics, they certainly qualify as fundamental theological principles.

5. 2 Tim. 3:16-17; 2 Pet. 1:20-21.

6. Liana Lupas and Erroll F. Rhodes, eds., *Scriptures of the World: A Compilation of the 2,167 Languages in Which at Least One Book of the Bible Has Been Published Since the Bible Was First Printed by Johannes Gutenberg* (London: United Bible Societies; New York: American Bible Society, 1996), 5–7.

7. David B. Barrett and Todd M. Johnson, "Annual Statistical Table on Global Mission: 1998," *International Bulletin of Missionary Research* 22, no. 1 (1998): 26–27.

8. Danielle Steel's website is located at http://www.randomhouse.com/features/steel/bookshelf.html; information retrieved spring 2002.

9. For the interested reader, excellent summaries of this research include F. F. Bruce, *The New Testament Documents: Are They Reliable?* (Downers Grove, Ill.: InterVarsity Press, 1997); and Josh McDowell, *Evidence That Demands a Verdict* (San Bernardino, Calif.: Here's Life Publishers, 1972), 13–78.

10. The most significant reason was to make a way by which people could be forgiven for their sins—an act of amazing grace that conveys volumes about the heart

of God. John 3:16; Rom. 3:22-24; Eph. 2:4-5, 8-9.

11. John 14:8.

12. John 14:9, NIV.

13. C. S. Lewis, *God in the Dock: Essays on Theology and Ethics* (Grand Rapids, Mich.: Eerdmans, 1970), 157–8.

14. C. S. Lewis, *Mere Christianity* (New York: Macmillan, 1969), 55–56.

Chapter Eleven: Soaring Free

1. 1 Thess. 5:23; Heb. 4:12, NIV.

2. The Ten Commandments were not intended to be a wet blanket on human activities but rather a standard of behavior that optimizes the quality of life. Exod. 20:1-17.

3. Rom. 1:18-23, New International Version.

4. Rom. 7:21-25, NIV.

5. Rom. 8:1-2, NIV, emphasis added.

6. The word *principles* would be the most commonly used word found in technical literature associated with aerodynamics. Since the word *law,* however, is often interchanged with the word *principle* in other areas of science, I have chosen to use the word *law* in order to retain the symmetry of the analogy.

7. 1 John 1:8-9, NIV.

8. Matt. 22:37; Mark 12:30.

9. Also see: Acts 2:37-38; Rom. 3:22-26; 10:9-13. Some might view this provision of grace as an excuse to sin all the more. The Bible anticipates such a distortion of the provision and warns against it in Romans 6:1-2 and 1 Thessalonians 4:6-7.

10. See chapter six, pages 78-80.

11. An eagle may not be keenly aware of the law of aero-dynamics in the same sense as the hang glider pilot, but experientially it does recognize its pattern of behavior and how to use it.

12. A thermal is a rising air current caused either by solar heating or by wind moving up the side of a mountain.

13. Acts 1:8; 1 Cor. 2:12-14, 3:16.

14. Gal. 5:22-23, NIV.

Chapter Twelve: Reasons for Hope

1. James Jeans, *The Mysterious Universe* (New York: Macmillan, 1944), 15.

2. Rom. 8:20-21, New International Version, emphasis added.

3. 1 Pet. 3:15, NIV.

4. For more on the evidence of the resurrection, see Josh McDowell, *Evidence That Demands a Verdict* (San Bernardino, Calif.: Here's Life Publishers, 1979), 179–260; F. F. Bruce, *The New Testament Documents: Are They Reliable?* (Downers Grove, Ill.: InterVarsity Press, 1997), 62–75.

5. 1 Thess. 4:13-18, NIV.

6. Rom. 8:11, NIV.

7. Rev.22:3, NIV.

8. Rev. 21:1-5, NIV, emphasis added.

9. John 20:19; Acts 1:9.

10. In fact, the story *is* true, having occurred in the family of a friend of a friend of mine.

11. The following is Lewis' statement: "I willingly believe that the damned are, in one sense, successful, rebels to the end; that the doors of hell are locked on the *inside.*" C. S. Lewis, *The Problem of Pain* (New York: Macmillan, 1962), 127.

12. Jesus told a parable that gives us a sobering glimpse into what it might be like to be in hell: Luke 16:19-31. See also God's judgment: Rom. 14:10; 2 Cor. 5:10.

13. Rom. 12:2, NIV.

14. Theologians term God's immediate declaration of a new believer as sin-free in his eyes "justification" (Rom. 3:21-26 NIV). They term the process of the

progressive defeat of our "bent" toward sin "sanctifica-
tion" (1 Thess. 5:23 NIV).

15. 1 John 1:8-9, NIV.

Conclusion

1. The New International Version is one such modern
English translation. It is the one most often quoted in
this book.

2. Gordon J. Van Wylen, *Thermodynamics* (New York:
Wiley, 1959). The comment I am referring to appears
on page 169, at the end of a chapter on the second law.

3. G. Campbell Morgan, *The Parables and Metaphors of
Our Lord* (New York: Revell, 1963), 15–16.

Printed in the United States
1073200003B